I WOKE TO FIND THAT
THE SOUND OF BREAKING GLASS
WAS REAL....

The nightmare that was climbing in my window was a lot worse than the one I'd dreamed. I was so astonished that I just watched as metal hands hooked onto the window frame and pulled the rest of the Machine into the room. Its camera was attached right about where a head would have been if it had been alive.

I vaulted out of bed and dashed for the door. I even managed to get the door partway open, but a metal hand seized my wrist and forced me to shut it again.

I turned to find the camera in my face. It wrenched me off my feet and threw me on the bed. The Machine scanned me for a moment, looking oddly human as it did so, then sharp blades came out of its fingertips....

SCORPIANNE

Scorpianne

Emily Devenport

A ROC BOOK

ROC
Published by the Penguin Group
Penguin Books USA Inc., 375 Hudson Street,
New York, New York 10014, U.S.A.
Penguin Books Ltd, 27 Wrights Lane,
London W8 5TZ, England
Penguin Books Australia Ltd, Ringwood,
Victoria, Australia
Penguin Books Canada Ltd, 10 Alcorn Avenue,
Toronto, Ontario, Canada M4V 3B2
Penguin Books (N.Z.) Ltd, 182–190 Wairau Road,
Auckland 10, New Zealand

Penguin Books Ltd, Registered Offices:
Harmondsworth, Middlesex, England

First published by Roc,
an imprint of Dutton Signet,
a division of Penguin Books USA Inc.

First Printing, August, 1994
10 9 8 7 6 5 4 3 2 1

 REGISTERED TRADEMARK—MARCA REGISTRADA

Printed in the United States of America

To my fellow members
of the Full Moon Club:
Rick Cook,
Peter L. Manly,
and Ernest Hogan

was feeling impatient near the end of that day, maybe because I was so close to retirement, the end of thirty-eight years of hard labor. But I wasn't tired, and my love of money was as strong as ever. So I punched *Lucy is in!* to the last customer inquiry and let him put his personal code through to my computer.

I watched my monitor as the requirements for Mr. 99876 came through. It was a long list, but once I recognized who he was I just glanced at it to make sure there were no changes. He was my old friend the Punisher. He liked me as a redhead.

I pulled on a long suc-vac wig and spray-tinted my pubic hair red. He liked me to start on the toilet, naked from the waist down. I gave my vulva a quick squirt from the slicker can and headed for the bathroom.

He always wanted the same thing. Here I am, taking a leak. I start playing with myself and he comes in and catches me at it. From there he bullies me over to the Machine.

I made my face go slack so I looked like the adolescent I was supposed to be. Make that horny adolescent. To get myself in the mood I thought about my money.

Stock portfolio. Money market. Mutual funds. Ooo! Aaah! Mmm!

Suddenly the camera came zipping in on its long, snaky cable and I heard the Punisher's voice— discreetly distorted, of course—through the speaker.

"Don't bother with that. Get on the Machine."

I gave him a nice pout, but obeyed pronto. I was more than happy to get it over with so I could call it a day and soak in my spa. I thought this guy must already have the electric vagina strapped on, so I hurried in to the Machine. The camera zipped after me.

The Machine bends into a hundred different "situations," but the Punisher liked a rear shot. So I stripped off my top, put my knees in the stirrups and my size 38E tits into the metal hands. I never grabbed the handlebars because I was too tall, so I grabbed the bar just above it. The Punisher used his joystick to elevate my augmented butt into the air and spread my legs. When my face was close to the ground I noticed that the repairmen had left the damned electrical cord exposed when they were there the day before. I made a mental note to file a complaint as soon as this session was over.

The electric penis snapped up like a cobra and poised at the ready. This was my cue to start panting with fear. But I knew perfectly well that the failsafe in the Machine would keep him from doing me any real harm. The trick is to make it *look* painful.

The Punisher began his usual shtick: "You've been a bad girl and I gotta punish you," and I was saying, "Please, I won't do it again," but thinking, *Christ, get on with it!* The camera circled the Machine as if he couldn't make up his mind what angle he wanted to watch from.

The penis snapped back and penetrated a lot harder than usual. I almost said *Christ!* out loud, but that would have been out of character, and I kept up my usual act even as the knee cups were spreading my legs a lot farther than they're supposed to go and the hands started to squeeze my artificial tits practically off. I didn't panic. I'm in great condition. I relaxed my vagina and reached for the control switch. I switched it to OFF.

The penis reared back and stopped. I was looking between my legs at it. The Punisher was giggling now. He said, "I'm going to give it to you like you've never had it before, cunt."

Clamps slid out of the leg bars and snapped shut on my lower legs. A pair came out of the handlebars too, but my hands were elsewhere, so they snapped shut on empty air. The camera circled 'round and 'round.

A blade came out of the tip of the penis. Razors also extended from the sides. The penis reared back and dove for my vagina, but I wrenched myself into a slightly different position and the knife sank into my (fortunately augmented) butt instead. I reached for the cord and pulled with everything I had while the penis stabbed my buns again and again. Blood splashed my face.

Then the penis began to slow down. The cord was out. Everything came to a stop.

Not a word from the Punisher. The camera withdrew to a corner and hovered there. I pulled my suc-vac wig off and gave the camera the finger.

"You're out of the club, Motherfucker!" I said and

threw the wig at it. It pulled the delicate camera off balance and sent it crashing to the floor. I tried to pretend it was the Punisher's head.

I told the paramedics to bring their tools. No way was I going to drag the Machine to the hospital with me.

Twenty-four hours later I came home with my butt in a sling and started making phone calls.

It had taken me a couple of hours to unscrew the bolts of the Machine from the floor mounts. I had dragged it along with me to the vidphone. If my legs hadn't had the biometal implants from the time I'd had them lengthened, they might have broken. I got them done the same time I got my tits and butt done. Added the face job and the youth padding under my skin the next year. Even though I had earned the money back a thousand times, it didn't please me that someone had damaged my expensive hide.

My first call was to Machine Co. I demanded to talk to the Complaint Department, but I got someone who was dressed too well to be a lackey. "What can I do for you, Ms. Cartier?" he asked me.

"I don't like the way your repairmen messed up my Machine," I said.

"I don't know what you mean."

"Well, here's the story. I'm suing you. I've had my injuries professionally corroborated and filed, and I've done the same for my Machine's nice little penile *enhancements*, and you know that's what it takes in court. But I'm willing to settle *out* of court. Make me an offer."

He was quiet for a moment. Then he said, "We don't respond graciously to threats."

"I'm not making any." I gave him a short silence like the one he had given me, but his poker face didn't change, so I continued. "Your Machine injured me. I'm putting in a legitimate claim. We're going to settle this out of court and then go our separate ways."

"Ah," he said. "One moment." The screen went blank for five minutes and then he was back. "Five hundred thousand," he said.

"I'll think about it. I'll get back to you in a few days." I severed the contact.

Had the repairmen put snoop devices in my apartment when they altered my Machine? I considered the next several calls I was going to make and decided it didn't matter if Machine Co. listened in. I would show them how well I could find things out while keeping my mouth shut at the same time. Maybe they would take the hint and up the ante before I came back with a counteroffer.

I'm not usually that stupid. But retirement was floating before my eyes like a lovely butterfly.

I went down the list of my acquaintances who owned Machines. It was a cottage industry, so about 99 percent of them should have been home. Only 70 percent of them answered. 11 percent more had their answering machines on, and the other 19 percent had been disconnected.

Someone else had to have put in a claim.

I chatted with each of the 70 percent, listening for any opportunity to talk about absent friends.

"I was thinking about doing a mother-daughter bit with Linda Tree," I told Wendy the hermaphrodite. "But I can't seem to get in touch with her."

"Haven't you heard?" Wendy said. "Linda's getting changed back. Gotta admit I'm glad to hear it. Her specialty gave me the creeps."

Now, I knew for a fact that Linda didn't have that kind of money. She had no business sense, and on top of that, she had a kid.

"I'd like to send her some flowers," I said.

"Designer Gene Co. You know, the one in Uptown." I sure did. The most expensive clinic in Arizona. Maybe in the whole Southwest.

"Thanks." I said good-bye to him/her.

I was really tired by then, but I made myself get up and take a good look at my apartment. I was sure that I couldn't take anything with me where I was going. No clothing or makeup; no food, since it might be poisoned. And certainly no mementos, much as that pained me. I hated to leave my books, my music, and the paintings I had so carefully collected over the past thirty years. But these days they can fit an awful lot of explosion into a very small space. And I certainly didn't want any locators on my person.

As I was locking my door, it suddenly occurred to me that I was very lucky they hadn't wired the lock to explode on me. They could have primed it to respond to my fingerprints, assuming they wanted to spend the money. That's what I was counting on, that they *didn't* want to spend it. I took my hands off the lock and started to turn, and that's when I first heard the footsteps.

The hall was tiled with marble, a holdover from old times when such things were considered fancy. My apartment was one door past the corner, and someone was walking up the other branch of the hallway, making an impossible sound. CLUNK—

CLUNK—CLUNK—CLUNK— Not the sound of a human foot at all.

I ran to the lift before my curiosity could get the better of me. The footsteps rounded the corner just as the doors opened, and I caught a glimpse of something white as I rushed in. The sound halted, as if the person had just seen me too. I pressed the LOBBY button before he could come any closer and zipped on down to the bottom floor, where I made my escape with very undignified haste.

I had planned to go directly to Designer Gene Co. to talk to Linda, but after the episode in the hall I decided to visit my old buddy Joe Santos instead. I had to ride the train, which made me almost vomit; but these occasional trips to Joe's were necessary. So I had to keep a stiff upper lip.

He was living in Glendale, running a legitimate gun shop up front and a not-so-legitimate one out back. He gave me a look full of high tension when I walked in. "Hello, *querida*," he said. "What do you need from me now?"

He was cutting his hair as short as I was then, a nice, crisp crew cut. It looked good on him. "I need a weapon," I said.

His nostrils flared. His ancestors must have been almost pure Castilian to give him nostrils like that. But another set of genes must have given him the black hair and eyes—those eyes that made me so nervous every time I had to come to him.

"Who's bothering you?" he asked.

"A whole bunch of people. In fact, a whole company."

He blinked, and I swear you could almost hear a

click. Then he walked around the counter and went to the front door. He closed it, locked it, and turned the GET LOST sign around. He came over to me very slowly and deliberately, and I tensed, waiting to see if he would try to do what I was always afraid he would do. Waiting to see if he would touch me. But he didn't. He just came real close and stared, eye to eye.

"Machine Co.?" he asked.

"Yes."

"You know they have system-wide connections? You know they have special customers in the government?"

"Of course they do. So do I."

"But none that would give you the sweat off their balls, I bet." He sneered, but I didn't take it personally. It was true.

"That's why I need a good gun. In fact, a force gun if you have one."

He smiled. His teeth were snow white. "Come on back," he said.

Joe loved weapons. He learned to love them when he was in the marines, killing rebels in the Mars Revolt. He still wore marine-issue fatigue pants and those sleeveless tees that showed off his build. "This baby looks like a projectile gun," he told me as we made our way through a dark, narrow hall to his inner sanctum. "Like a fat thirty-eight."

"Just for curiosity's sake, how many years will I get if I'm caught with it?"

"Thirty-eight!" he said, and laughed. "No, just kidding, *querida*. You'd get twenty. Parole in ten."

"Wonderful."

"I wouldn't let them have you. I've got connections too."

I knew that. That's why I indulged myself with his friendship, despite his need to do what I couldn't stand. I'll be damned if I know why he put up with *me*.

"You still in the business?" he asked me as he unlocked the door.

"Not anymore. As of yesterday."

He looked at me over his shoulder, his hands still working. "But I bet you keep a few customers. Just for fun."

"No."

"Really?" He got the door open and moved aside, like he expected me to brush past him. "Not even your Joselito?"

I didn't move. I didn't answer, either. It was an old argument, one that had been going on ever since I took him off my client list. He had pirated his way into my system, and kept coming back after I told him to go to hell. He said he liked my spirit. I liked his too, I even started to enjoy it a little; but the whole thing began to get scary the day he showed up on my doorstep. I don't like to remember that day.

The room past the doorway was pitch black, as black as Joe's eyes. "You know what I think?" he said. "I think if you let someone touch you—just a little at a time—you'd get used to it. That's how they cure phobias."

"I can't do that."

He turned so that the door was a dark frame behind him. His movements were as controlled and smooth as a snake's.

"I know you can't," he said. "But I like to think

about it." He reached out with one hand and brushed a wall sensor. The room behind him turned brilliant white. "C'mon in." He went into the room without looking to see if I followed.

The room was loaded to the rafters with contraband, but it wasn't as disordered as it looked. All of the explosives were stored in their separate neutral components, and none of the guns were loaded. He went to a wall and pulled an ordinary-looking gun off the rack. "Custom-made," he said, touching the piece with a lover's hands. "And it's a silent little monster. All you'll hear is the crackle of the beam through the atmosphere. And the scream." He laughed shortly.

"How many times can I fire it before the clip runs out?"

"Pack," he said. "Force guns don't have clips. If you set it on low, you can fire it fifty times. That'll knock a man down and gave him a first-degree burn. If you set it on high, you'll have ten shots. That'll blow a man apart and char most of his body to the bone."

He said it in a matter-of-fact tone, like a doctor talking about a surgical procedure he's done a thousand times. He extended the weapon to me.

"Hold it, *querida*."

I managed to take the gun without touching his hand. He moved closer, but Joe had given me guns before, and he needed to be that close to show me how to fire it. I could stand that.

"Here's the safety." He indicated an L-shaped groove with its switch at the top of the L. "Better keep that on unless you're going to shoot. Don't want it to go off and burn your pretty toes. Practice flipping it on, because you want to be able to do it fast."

I did, five times. My hands are strong, so I was able to do it to his satisfaction.

"To shoot, you squeeze the trigger, just like you would a projectile gun. But the kick isn't as big. Now, slap in the pack."

He showed me where it went, and I got it in the first time.

"Good. Come on out back."

The yard behind the shop was a large dirt plot with twenty-foot walls. He had the place rigged with anti-spy devices and camouflaged with holographic projectors. There were some straw dummies set up on the far side, in front of explosion absorbers, the kind you'd find on a regular shooting range. He could have just painted targets on the absorbers, but for some reason he really liked those dummies.

"Shoot," he said.

I did, almost as fast as he said it. I burned the head off one of the dummies. The beam made more of a hum than a crackle.

"That's the maximum range, for this gun," he said. "Fifty feet. You can shoot as close as five, but if you get too close you're gonna get burned yourself."

"All right."

He smiled. "Is that all you want this time? You wanna talk about pay?"

"One more thing. I'd like you to see if there are any credit tracers on me."

He nodded, and we went back into the inner sanctum.

Joe had a very expensive computer, the top of the line. It was so powerful he had to take careful steps to hide the power drain. He got into the credit net and played around with the keyboard for a while, his eyes reading faster than I could follow.

I stood behind him and admired the play of muscles across his shoulders. He was like one of my paintings, beautiful to look at. He was youngish, like me, but if you looked closely, you could see paler areas in his olive skin, testifying to eighteen months he had spent in a regeneration tank after the war. He didn't need youth padding.

"Yep," he said. "They're looking for you. I'll establish a new line for you. What name do you want?"

I was stumped. I'd never had to go underground before. I had always been a legitimate businesswoman, except for occasional dealings with Joe.

"I know," he said. "Querida Amore. That's your new name. Remember to sign it with an *e* on the end of 'Amore.' "

"Right," I promised.

He made me a credit disk on another one of his illegal machines and dug up a second pack for me, and a shoulder holster. After a critical look at my hospital-issue coveralls, he pulled out an old leather jacket too. The jacket smelled like him. I placed it all on his cluttered desk and waited for him to claim his price. It wasn't money.

What Joe always wanted was a kiss. Not just an ordinary kiss, but a very slow and complicated one. It was almost more than I could stand, but I permitted it because he did things for me no one else would or could.

This time he started from behind. I felt his fingers on the nape of my neck, but just barely. The youth padding had reduced my sensitivity considerably, which was a part of the reason I had wanted it. In another moment I felt his breath there too, and then his hand on my stomach, and his body pressed up against mine.

By then I was shaking. I tried closing my eyes, but that just made it worse, shut me into a dark place where all I could think about was the touching. So I focused on his gun rack instead.

His other hand slid over my shoulder and down my arm, then up the front of my body to my breasts, the two places not covered by youth padding. He touched both of them, lingering over the nipples, until I was breathing so fast the back of my throat began to burn. I had to do that. If I started to vomit, I wouldn't be able to stop.

His mouth brushed my neck and then my ear. His hand cupped my chin and turned my head until I was looking right into his eyes. I thought I could see electrical arcs in his pupils. I took one last deep breath, and then he kissed me. But that wasn't even all of it.

He started very light, barely pressing his lips against mine. He pulled my chin far up and back, until I was forced to turn my body against his to ease the strain on my neck. He slid one arm around the small of my back and pulled me tight against him, stroking my short hair with his other hand. His tongue slipped into my mouth.

Just when I thought I would lose it, he withdrew his tongue, his lips, and then his body. And the amazing thing was that it had all been one very long, very smooth motion, from start to finish.

"Baby, you kiss better than most people fuck," he said. But at least he wasn't smiling. His face was like a statue's as he watched me pick up my stuff with shaking hands.

"I'll walk you to the door," he said.

All I could do was nod.

"Call me if you need more than a gun, *querida*," he said at the door.

"I will." But I worried about the price. I thought it might be more than a kiss next time.

But I felt calmer as I walked away, even though I knew he was watching me. Being watched never bothered me, and I supposed he had been partly right about getting used to being touched. It still made me sick, but I seemed to get over it faster than I used to.

I had to get on the underground train again. I hadn't done that more than six times in my whole life, I hated it so much. There were perverts in there who liked to brush up against people, even stand with their bodies touching yours if they could get away with it. But I was lucky to hit one of the empty hours, and the people riding with me seemed as eager to keep their distance as I was.

I was able to tolerate the train long enough to get to Tempe, where I had never shopped before. I found a store that catered to my I'm-a-butch,-stay-the-hell-away-from-me-or-I'll-cut-you tastes. I bought something that went nicely with Joe's jacket and thanked the gods of fashion that it was December. Even the temperature domes over the city wouldn't have been able to shut out an Arizona summer completely.

I jumped a private taxi to Uptown. It let me out right in front of Designer Gene Co.

It had been built in the Edwardian Revival, so it

was pretty peculiar-looking, especially next to all of the Aztecan and Spanish Colonial stuff that had been built back when they used to have that law about Southwestern architecture. I rather liked the hodge-podge effect.

I stood in the elegant, sterile lobby while they called up to Linda's room and asked if she would see me. I was a little surprised by how quickly she said yes.

"Go on up, dear," said the youngish nurse in her gentle Southern accent. "She's real happy to have a visitor. Tell the lift you want 517-A."

"I'll do that." I gave her my best smile, which she eagerly returned.

On the way up, I took some time to meditate and regulate my breathing, so I wouldn't look too shocked when I saw Linda's wounds. Linda Tree was thirty-seven, but she had the body of a nine-year-old. She also had the business sense of a nine-year-old, or she would have been comfortably retired by then.

I had wondered if she could recognize me with short hair, but she recognized me just fine. It was I who could barely recognize her. She looked like she had been run over by a lawn mower. She managed to get one puffy eye open and focus it on me.

"Lucy?" she said. "How the hell are you?"

"My Machine knifed me in the butt. How are you?"

She closed the eye. "Now I know how hamburger feels," she said.

And I knew how it *looked*. "How much are you suing Machine Co. for?"

She got so still I was almost tempted to check for

a pulse. But then the eye opened again and glared at me.

"You're a heartless bitch, Lucy. A greedy, heartless—"

"Thank you. I work hard at it. But I have a long way to go before I reach the Machine Co. level, don't you think?"

Linda shuddered. Maybe she was thinking about the customer who had done her. He must have been a doctor to know how to inflict so much damage without killing.

"They're giving me five hundred thousand," she said.

"You're kidding. Is that all?"

"I don't want to fight about it. I can change back to a woman's body now."

"You should get a lot more." I turned and presented my injured butt. "I'm getting five hundred thou. For *this*. You should be getting four times that!"

"Don't you get it?" Her voice rose almost to a normal level. I think she was trying to scream. "Our Machines were supposed to kill us! They're snuff Machines!"

I had thought that was pretty obvious. What wasn't so obvious was how much of a settlement would be *too* much. If I had to settle for five hundred thou and my life, I'd take it.

"You didn't even try to get more?" I asked.

"Look," she said. "You know my kid, Tracy? She's nine now. The age I look. She thinks it's okay to have sex over the vid with grown men because that's what Mommy does. The other day I caught her playing with my Machine—."

She went on for a while. I didn't know why the

hell anyone in this business would want to have kids anyway, but I didn't say so. When she was done, I said, "That's tough."

"I've been trying to explain to her about puberty. How she's going to grow breasts and have a period one day. She doesn't want to believe it. She gets so upset she wets her bed."

"Sounds like she could use some expensive therapy."

Linda's chest rose and fell slightly, her version of a sigh. "I'm pretty tired now," she said. "I think you'd better go."

I took a few steps backward, meaning to just turn and go. But seeing her so helpless kind of tugged at my conscience. "Linda," I said, "have you heard any weird footsteps outside your door?"

"Weird footsteps?"

"Really loud ones. Like CLUNK CLUNK CLUNK?"

The part of her mouth that wasn't covered with bandages frowned. "Once I have my medicine, I don't hear *anything*. In fact, I think it's almost time for another dose. Ask the nurse for me, will you? On your way out?"

"Yeah," I said. "Good luck, Linda."

As I went out the door I thought I heard her say, "Good luck," but I wasn't sure if she meant it for me or if she was mocking me. I told the nurse in the lobby about the medicine.

"Coming right up!" she said, like the perkiest little waitress you ever saw.

It was dark when I walked out of Designer Gene Co. I almost took another taxi to the Hilton, but paranoia made me stop and think about it. Linda seemed to be okay; she hadn't been silenced for asking for a settlement. On the other hand, they had her where they wanted her.

I looked up and down the street, at the well-dressed crowds and glittering buildings, and I felt eyes watching me from all directions.

So I forced myself back onto the underground train to Glendale instead. That place was so run-down, they hadn't even bothered to extend the weather dome over it. A lot of people there couldn't afford even the most primitive Youth Technology available, and they actually looked their age. Glendale was so dilapidated that most of the government spy devices had probably shorted out years ago. And those that hadn't were done in by Joe and his type.

Run-down as it was, it had malls just like any other part of town. I went into a Frilly's and started shopping around for a new identity. Hair, clothes, and makeup. I marched in looking like a commando and came out again with mincing little steps, in a feminine suit with a short skirt, my hair long and auburn, my face as vapid as a high-priced fashion model's.

Joe's jacket was hidden in the bag with my new stuff. Just sentimental, I guess.

From there I found a Motel 62 and checked into a room that was every bit as cheap as the name suggests. I hated it, but I was asleep the moment I hit the bed, my wounded butt pointing toward the heavens.

I woke up with a stiff neck and sore breasts from sleeping on my stomach, and of course my ass ached like hell, despite my attempts to stay off it. Some yoga and low-impact aerobics took care of the former, and some low-grade codeine from the gift shop at the hotel reduced the latter to a tolerable throbbing.

I ordered breakfast from room service and keyed the room vid into the news net. I wanted to see if anyone I knew had been found dead.

When the knock came, I started toward the door and then froze with my hand on the knob.

"Just a moment," I said, and concealed the force gun under my robe. "Come in!"

An adolescent girl wheeled my tray in. Her eyes widened when she saw me—I still had my wig and my persona in place.

"Are you a model?" she asked me.

"Yes," I said, in my coolest snob tone. Her face got a little stiff and her eyes narrowed, which told me that either she was offended or she was a better actress than me.

"Your tip's on the dresser." I pretended to fuss over the tray while I really watched her out of the corner of my eye. She scooped the money up and hurried out, her ass twitching in a haughty fashion.

The news net was full of murders, but no Machines were mentioned. I was intrigued to note that a small-scale war had occurred on Ganymede between the asteroid miners and the merchants who sucked a fortune out of them. I don't think anyone was surprised by that one.

After a couple of hours it all started to get boring, so I dressed myself up, hopped a private taxi to Tempe, and called Wendy the hermaphrodite from a public com.

No one answered.

I stood there and let it buzz twenty times. Her/his answering service wasn't even on. Images of stabbing penises and clawing, metal hands were running through my head. But it all seemed kind of abstract. If I really wanted to know what had happened, I figured, I'd better go and see for myself. Besides, Wendy might be alive but unable to reach her/his vidphone.

I looked for a private taxi that would take me to Phoenix. I could feel Joe's gun under my arm, under the spider-silk blazer, and another small portion of my mind was wondering how fast I could draw it. I think I must have hypnotized myself a little bit, because I was out of the taxi and up the steps to Wendy's apartment building before I knew it.

The computer in the lobby glared down at me from its perch over the security door. "Whom do you wish to see?" it asked me in a neutral, sexless voice.

"Wendy Dionisius," I said, and the door immediately opened. Wendy had an open-door policy for absolutely anyone who wanted to see her/him, even door-to-door salesmen and religious nuts. I rode up the lift to the eighteenth floor and stepped out into a thickly carpeted hallway.

No one was in sight, and when I walked to Wendy's door my feet made no sound at all.

Wendy's door was always unlocked. I opened it and peeked into her/his living room.

Jazz trickled in from the kitchen. She/he liked to leave it on all the time so people would go in and make themselves comfortable, maybe make themselves a snack. I didn't go in there just yet. I closed the front door behind me and moved cautiously into the living room.

I had been there only once, maybe ten years earlier, but the place hadn't changed at all. The wall over the fireplace was papered with every greeting card Wendy had ever received, from the sappy to the insulting. She/he loved them all. I even recognized a few I had sent.

The Christmas tree was up, just as it was all year round, and the presents under it threatened to crowd out everything else in the room. There were several for me. Just the week before, she/he had called me up and said, "You know my rule! If you want your presents, you have to come over and get them yourself, give me a proper visit. Don't worry about the crowd, love. I'll make a private appointment for you."

I had promised I would try. And now here I was.

I poked my head into the kitchen. Bowls of imported chocolates and candy sat on the kitchen table. A big hand-drawn sign on the fridge said, HELP YOURSELF!

Somehow it had the look of a place that had been

deserted years ago. I backed out of the kitchen and tiptoed through the living room, down the hall to the office. The office door was closed, so I put my ear to it.

I heard the hum of a Machine that was on, but at rest. My heart was pounding. I put my hand on the knob, turned it, and slowly opened the door.

Wendy was in there. I stared for a moment, and then vomited up breakfast.

Wendy's Machine had been designed for much more complex functions than mine had. It now resembled some sort of hideous insect. It had torn Wendy's penis right off, and what was left was hanging from a gloved metal hand like a hunk of abused liver. His/her breasts had been sliced off with razor-sharp blades, but that wasn't how Wendy had died. Another metal hand was locked around his/her throat, and from the way the eyes and tongue bulged, I guessed that Wendy had been strangled slowly.

I couldn't help but take note of the way his/her wrists and ankles were bleeding, testifying to the struggle he/she had put up. Looking at them made me so angry I started to vomit again, even though nothing was left in my stomach. I was on my knees by then, with my hair in my face, so I had no idea how much of a show I had put on until I looked up again and saw the camera, not two feet away from me.

The john who had murdered her was still plugged into the system.

The camera moved a little closer, scanning my body. I sat there with a blank face for a moment, as if I could never make a dangerous move, then whipped out the force gun. I was happy to see the camera start back, like the john had forgotten he wasn't really there.

"I know why you killed her!" I said. "You were jealous that her dick was bigger than yours!"

And I pulled the trigger. The gun was set on maximum, so the camera disintegrated. It had probably given the john a nice roar of static before his screen went blank. Unfortunately, that was the best I could do.

I was angry enough to call the police at that point, but that would have been absurd. The john who killed Wendy may have been a policeman himself. So I washed my face in the bathroom and exited the apartment, sure that the only killer around had been the one in the system.

As I was about to get onto the lift, I heard a sound in the hall. Something scuffling on the carpet.

No one was there except me—unless there was a corner I couldn't see, out of sight down at the far end. I drew the force gun again, making sure the safety was off, and pressed myself against the wall.

"Who's there?" I called.

No one answered, but I felt someone listening.

"Are you looking for me? Why don't you just come out and talk to me instead of hiding like a frightened little dick-head?" I figured that would offend a macho-minded assassin. Unless he was an ice cube.

"I know you're following me, and I know who sent you. So why don't you just come out and we'll talk about it. Maybe we can cut our own deal."

Something white leaped around the corner, and I fired. It burst into flames and sank to the floor.

I blinked. It was a piece of white—clothing? Where was the body? It should have been lying there smoldering. The wall behind it had a hole the size of a basketball, revealing pipes and fused wiring. I took a step forward, and realization hit me like a brick between the eyes.

It was a sheet. The guy who threw it was still hiding on the other side of the corner, and now he knew I had a force gun.

I turned and ran into the lift. And when I got to the lobby, I ran through it without pausing to see if anyone was coming down in the other lift, slipped and almost fell on the polished marble on my way out. I hopped a taxi, ran back to my little hotel room, then tucked myself into a corner and banged myself on the forehead, chanting, "Stupid, stupid, stupid!"

An hour later I wasn't any smarter, but I did have one hell of a headache.

After thirty-eight years as a high-priced prostitute I knew an awful lot about protecting the identity of my customers but very little about protecting my own. I must have lain on that bed in Motel 62 for hours, considering and rejecting lame plans of action.

My first thought had been to switch hotels. But if someone had trailed me back there, they could certainly trail me anywhere else. There was only one man I knew who had ever succeeded in "disappearing" without getting killed in the process. And if I wanted him to do the same for me, he would probably want some substantial and prolonged touching in return. In fact he would probably want to fuck.

I actually let my mind linger over that possibility. I suppose I was curious about the repulsion I felt for real sex. I wasn't alone; just about everyone had some sort of Machine these days. But there was a time, at the beginning, when I did my clients in person.

I started at sixteen. I would tell you what drove me to it, except that I don't remember. I lost most of my memory when I was in the hospital being treated for a lovely little disease, fondly referred to as the Blue Clap. The Blue Clap was said to have originated on Mars, born from a combination of engineered life-forms and illicit sex.

One image I had begun to remember lately was the doctor leaning over my bed, his face stiff with horror and pity. "They've spread throughout your lymph system," he told me. "Almost every gland in your body is infected. We've managed to halt the progress to your brain, but we're going to have to remove the parasites practically one by one—"

"Will I ever be able to have children?" I asked him, and I remember that my tone was pleading. I can't imagine why I would have wanted such a thing, but the memory is there.

He rubbed his face, looking very tired. "Miss Cartier," he said, "I can't guarantee you're even going to survive this process. I would place your odds somewhere around fifty-fifty."

The parasites were wormlike, and they caused terrible pain as they grew. Theoretically they would have grown until my major organs shut down and my body bloated up and turned blue; then they would have lived in my dead carcass until it was completely eaten and they could fly away to the next stage of their metamorphosis.

My own metamorphosis consisted of the removal of several major organs as well as my breasts, uterus, and ovaries. Once the parasites were gone, I went into regeneration for sixteen months. That's when I lost most of my memory.

"You can have children now," the doctor informed me, smiling warmly. His hands, as he helped me out of the tank, caused me to cringe.

"Thank you, doctor," I said, wondering what the hell he was talking about.

You can't imagine how liberating it is not to have parents, not to have a childhood full of pain and failure. I was born on the halfshell, emerged from the foam on the ocean.

Picturing myself in Botticelli's painting made me laugh out loud. I switched on the news net, popped a couple more codeines, and settled in for some serious information gathering.

I tuned in right in the middle of an update of the Ganymede micro-war. I knew that was what it was because the announcer was saying, "Ten thousand dead and another fifteen thousand missing. The Hermes Transport Company has suspended all long-range transport until further notice; but experts are predicting the miners will run out of food and water within the week. Oxygen may run out even sooner—"

They were showing footage of the wrecked merchant zone, ruptured domes and bodies that looked almost as if they had been frozen from the inside out, instantaneously. I wondered if those grimacing faces had been burned black by blasters first, or if the cold did it.

"Miners have requested terms from Hermes officials still on Ganymede—" said the announcer, and the scene shifted to an underground bunker full of dirty, desperate people who obviously had never had the benefit of Youth Technology. A female miner was holding a handcuffed man with a torn suit and bloody face, but there was no audio with the vid, so I could only guess what she was saying. I assumed it had something to do with murder. "—but Hermes officials of Earth are refusing to negotiate until all hostages are released. It is estimated that over ten billion dollars in fines will have to be paid before miners will be allowed to regain their former jobs—"

Looking at the desperate face of that female miner, I wondered if I was seeing the beginning of a new class of space worker: the slave. It sure didn't look like the miners were going to get the better conditions they had risked everything for. As ruthless as they had been, Hermes was apparently a lot more ruthless. Personally, I would have accepted that as a given from the very beginning.

The program had cut back to more footage of dead people, and the announcers were droning on about the number of children estimated dead. I was wishing they would go on to something else. I thought about turning it off, but I couldn't move. Something was nagging at the back of my mind, distracting me.

Why didn't you warn him/her? it demanded.

On the vid, a tiny, burned head was sticking above a pile of bodies.

You could have warned Wendy not to use her/his Machine. Why didn't you do it?

"I had to look after myself," I said. I always did that. I was the center of my world—that was the only way to survive.

You knew there was a possibility her/his Machine might be rigged, just like yours.

"I didn't even think about it!" I scrubbed my face, trying to rub out the images on the vid of crying faces, people on the other satellites who were worried about missing relatives.

Why didn't you think about it?

"Why would they rig *all* of the Machines?" I wondered. "They can't kill *all* prostitutes. Even they couldn't get away with that."

On the vid, an executive was talking in a dry, slightly superior tone about the changes that would obviously need to be made in the future. "We're going to spend much more of our budget on security, I can tell you that," he announced.

They can get away with anything. Absolutely anything.

"What amazes me," said the voice of an expert on labor relations, "is that the miners didn't revolt two hundred years ago, back when the asteroid mining frontier was still so open, so unregulated. For heaven's sake, they wrangle asteroids! If they had decided to slingshot a few of those in the wrong direction— we're talking about a couple million megatons of explosive force on impact!"

That got my attention. Suddenly Wendy was thrust into the background again as I was forced to think about the safety of my own hide. But apparently nothing further was going to be said about the miners, at least during this cast, and they were already segueing back into Earth news.

I don't know why I didn't warn him/her, I told the

voice inside me. *And I don't think I want to know.* It was silent after that, possibly tired out from struggling against the current of my self-concern.

With all of that going on elsewhere, no one was spending much time on the little murders that may have occurred overnight in Phoenix. Not even on the local news net, which I listened to for an hour or so. I did find out that the Phoenix Art Museum was hosting an exhibit of Cyberealists starting the next day, and I was so busy wondering if I could possibly contrive some way to get to it without being observed that a piece of information almost slipped past me.

"Have you seen this person?" said the perky newswoman, and a photo of Wendy flashed on the screen. "Wendy Dionisius has been missing since yesterday, according to good friends. Police are not suspecting foul play at this point, but anyone who knows the whereabouts of Ms. Dionisius is strongly urged to call 622-911 immediately."

The recorded image of another woman popped onto the screen. "It just isn't like Wendy," she said. "She *never* leaves her apartment. Not without letting me know where she's going, anyway!"

This woman droned on for another minute about Wendy, but I could already tell she had never met her/him.

I got up from the bed, and a wave of dizziness swept over me. I was probably taking too much codeine. I went out to the street and hopped a taxi to the Glendale Mall. This time I went into a joint called Trashers. When I came out again, my hair was chin-length and black, my clothing was leather, and I had managed to bind my boobs into the C+ category.

I hopped a taxi to Phoenix, to Wendy's apartment. Perhaps four hours had passed since I had found her.

"Whom do you wish to see?" asked the computer.

"Wendy," I said, then dashed into the lift as soon as the door opened. I figured I had maybe fifteen minutes, tops, to get in and out before they came to pick me up.

Wendy's apartment was empty. The tree was gone, the cards were gone, the candy and chocolates, and of course the Machine and Wendy. The carpet smelled like it had just been cleaned, and the walls smelled the same.

I dashed out again, but this time I headed for the underground train. The place was crowded with people. I was jostled and pushed, but managed to navigate myself into a relatively uncrowded car without vomiting or fainting. I thought Joe would have been proud of me.

By the time I got back to my hotel I was sick, exhausted, and blond. I fell asleep, but unfortunately forgot to lie on my stomach. I woke up with my ass throbbing hard enough to knock me right out of bed.

I turned over, took some codeine, and went back to sleep.

Maybe I should have skipped the codeine, because I had one hell of a dream. It started out well enough, with me floating, free of pain, my worries so far away that I would hardly remember that I had any.

But then I began to realize I really *was* floating, in that regeneration tank from long ago. It was full of sunset-colored fluid. That was pretty, anyway. I could open my eyes under the water and see people and things dimly through the glass. The people looking at me. I fancied I could even hear their voices dimly through the glass and the fluid. I was sure they were discussing me.

"Lucy. Lucy Cartier. Sixteen years old. Born on Mars. Left at the age of sixteen, after regeneration treatment for the Blue Clap. I can't guarantee you're even going to survive this process. I would place your odds somewhere around fifty-fifty."

Are the parasites gone? I wondered with a flash of panic. But they must be gone. My body felt so good, so new. I flexed my muscles and felt something odd. They were so little. *I* was so little. I looked down at myself, and tried to scream with my mouth full of fluid.

I was a fetus.

Born on the halfshell, my own voice told me, as if trying to comfort me. *You were born on the halfshell.* But I didn't want to make sense of the words. Instead I pounded on the tank with my tiny fists until I saw cracks, and the sound of shattering glass filled my ears.

I woke to find that the sound of breaking glass was real and the nightmare that was climbing through my window was a lot worse than the one I had dreamed on my own. I was so astonished, I just watched as metal hands hooked onto the window frame and pulled the rest of the Machine into the room. Its camera was attached right about where a head would have been if it had been alive. It swiveled toward me and paused.

I was still dressed in my last getup, blond wig and all. For one moment I harbored the futile hope that it would think I was the wrong woman. But it started after me the moment it saw me, pulling three more pairs of limbs into the room.

I vaulted out of bed and dashed for the door. I heard the sound of hydraulic limbs moving right behind me. I even managed to get the door part way open, but a metal hand seized my wrist and forced me to shut it again.

I turned to find the camera right in my face. I guess I went into my act automatically, I don't think I made a conscious decision about it. My face softened into that dreamy look my customers had loved for so many years, and I breathed, "What do you want?"

I was wrenched off my feet and carried to the bed. This Machine was a hundred times more flexible than the one I'd had at home, and its hands were more sensitive too. It gripped me just hard enough to hold tight but not hard enough to bruise. It threw me onto the bed and seized me again when I tried to get away.

It scanned me for a moment, looking oddly human as it did so, then withdrew one pair of hands from my body. Sharp blades came out of its fingertips. It took every ounce of acting ability I had to keep still as those blades came toward me. I didn't want to give the operator the satisfaction of seeing me scream. At least not yet.

But the blades didn't scratch me. Instead they carefully cut my jumpsuit from my body. The camera took a full minute to scan me again before it cut off my underwear and bra, too. Then it began to touch me with those sensitive hands, and I was startled by how warm they were. They must have been wired for heat. That gave me a moment of terror as I realized that warm could easily become hot.

I expected it to go right for my breasts and my vagina, but it touched me all over, my face, my hair, my elbows and knees, even lingering over my feet, before getting to my breasts and stimulating my nipples so skillfully that I immediately thought of Joe. I gasped, and the camera swiveled up to my face, watching me as it continued to rub and tease, and I began to get an odd suspicion. As the camera hovered over my mouth, I almost said, "Joe?"

While one pair of hands kept busy with my breasts, another pair was stroking my thighs and probing between my legs. I was wet there, which was no big surprise. After thirty-eight years I could get wet just by thinking about it. That's what I thought then.

"Who are you?" I asked, and was surprised at the tremor in my voice. One of the hands touched my mouth, gently. The Machine shifted its position until a boxlike arrangement was over my pelvis, and the penis slid out. It was large, one of the ten-inch models, and it had a clitoral stimulator just above it. Two pairs of hands held my pelvis and legs in position while the penis began to work on me, slowly and gently at first, and then with increasing intensity. I couldn't help but respond. My whole body was shaking by the time I climaxed, and I didn't have to fake the groans.

The penis finished me off skillfully, then withdrew. I lay there gasping for several moments until I noticed that the Machine wasn't moving anymore. Its camera was fixed on my face. I looked at it and braced myself—I wasn't sure for what.

"Did you like that, bitch?" asked an undistorted voice.

A woman's voice.

"Who are you?" I asked again.

"Who are you, who are you!" she mocked. "Stupid whore. This really is all you're good for."

I had my breath again, and my tremors had subsided, leaving me more exhausted than I could ever remember feeling. So I was calm when I asked, "And now you're going to kill me?"

"I'm going to kill you in person," she said.

That set bells off in my head until I thought I might have a stroke. But I kept my voice level.

"You make love like a pro," I said.

She didn't answer.

"At least tell me one thing. Are you going to kill me for Machine Co.?"

"What difference does it make? Yeah, why not. I've received checks from them. From someone else too, someone you don't remember. Let's see if that'll keep your little brain busy for a while."

The Machine withdrew from me and crawled back to the window. I couldn't resist asking one more question.

"Why did you make love to me?"

Its head swiveled in my direction as it was climbing out the window. "I thought you should have a little fun before you die. You have one hour to get out of here." It started to leave again, then seemed to change its mind. "Why shouldn't I tell you?" asked the voice. "I'm Scorpianne. See you in fifty-nine minutes, Lucy."

And it disappeared. I heard the hydraulic sound of its limbs climbing away from the window, and then nothing.

I jumped up and stuffed everything I owned into

my shopping bags and got dressed, my limbs feeling like lead. I left the hotel without settling my bill and hailed a taxi; but I forgot to tell the electronic driver where I wanted to go, so it took me to its last destination, another shopping mall in Glendale. I paid it and stumbled into the mall. I couldn't decide what to do next.

Finally I went to a com and called the only number I could think of.

"Joe," I said, "come get me."

t wasn't my Machine," said Joe. "I do my raping in person."

We were alone together in the cabin of a light aircraft, flying somewhere over the Arizona desert. I didn't know where we were going and I didn't care. I could feel him looking at me from time to time, but I couldn't read his expression.

He had come to fetch me at the mall as casually as a father picking up his daughter, except that he had to take my arm and steer me to his private transport, I was so dazed. I didn't even mind the touch that much. And now we were flying nowhere together. It was a big relief.

The desert landscape soothed my visual needs, if nothing else. The sun was setting and taking a very long time to do it, turning the mountains red; and even after the sun had dropped below the horizon, the light persisted, deepening the purples and browns. "Are we going to your Fortress of Solitude?" I asked Joe, imaging a tower carved out of red rock.

He handed me a box of tissues. I stared at them blankly. He pulled one out and dabbed my cheek. The tissue came away wet. I was crying.

"I feel sick," I told him.

"Your face is flushed." He glanced at me, his handsome features seeming almost pleased. Maybe he liked seeing me do such a female thing as crying. Maybe he liked rescuing me. I was fortunate that he did.

"I miss my money and my paintings," I said, and was rewarded with a twisting in my gut of genuine regret. Thirty-eight years of hard work. I had wanted to retire on Mykonos, a beautiful, unspoiled Greek island. I had imagined that I would walk along the beach, and in that remote part of the world I would have glimpsed the Mountains of the Gods. I would have taken trips to Delos and looked at the Archaic stone lions.

"Money is just electricity on the screen," said Joe. "I can get you all you want."

"Right," I said. "And in return I can be your dumb little friend, always at your beck and call. Whatever you want goes, and whatever I want depends on what kind of mood you're in. What do you think I am, a pros—"

I stopped, astonished at what I had been about to say, and began to laugh. It felt good at first, but I couldn't stop. I was laughing like a maniac, and Joe was laughing too, caught up in his own madness.

Finally we were both too exhausted to do anything but grin like loons. "The hooker and the soldier," Joe said. "We were made for each other."

The sky was filled with naked stars now. I had never seen them that way—not that I could remember, anyway. The stars on the dome were simulated. I wondered if the stars in the Mykonos sky looked this way.

Joe was turning the plane, and a mountain loomed

black in the windshield. Then we were past it and dipping toward blinking red stars lined up below us. I felt the dropping-elevator effect in my stomach as the lights got bigger. He touched the plane down, light as a feather, coasted several hundred feet, and brought it to a stop.

There was some bluish-white light shining off to my right, but I couldn't make out where it was coming from. Joe jumped out of his side of the airplane and went around to mine, opening the door for me and helping me out as if I were a rich old lady going to her favorite bistro. As soon as I got up, my butt gave me a twinge, as if to say, *Remember me?*

We walked toward the light. I couldn't tell if it was coming from a building or from the mountain itself; then I realized they were the same thing. The building was *inside* the mountain. We were walking toward a recessed doorway, and someone was standing in front of the light, waiting for us.

"You really do have a Fortress of Solitude," I whispered to Joe. "Who are you people, anyway?"

"We're dead," he said. "It doesn't matter who we are."

As we got closer, I realized the figure was female. She was standing with her arms crossed. We stepped inside the rocky enclave, and she retreated in front of us, backing into the light. She was youngish, had short brown hair and a pleasant, intelligent face with gray eyes that were looking at Joe, seeming to want to avoid me completely.

"I'm the only one here right now," she told him.

"You're the one we need to see," he said and typed a code into a keyboard on the wall. The door slid shut, making my ears pop.

She nodded and finally looked at me. "You're Lucy," she said.

"Yes."

"I'm Ann." She held out her hand and I made myself shaking it. At least I knew Joe hadn't told her *everything* about me.

"She's sick," said Joe. "She needs a full exam."

"You're a doctor?" I asked Ann.

She nodded. "I used to work for Designer Gene Co. Before my death. Come on back this way. We'll have a look at you."

She started down the hall. I looked at Joe, and he nodded. "She's okay. She and I go back a long time."

Ann glanced over her shoulder at Joe, her eyes brimming over with an emotion that any fool could read. Then she looked at me and beckoned. "Come on," she said. "I've got a hunch I know what's wrong."

"Your doctors were excellent," said Ann as she ran a sensor over my breasts. "They managed to reattach every nerve."

The inside of my boobs glared at me from the monitor, the bioimplants two large and slightly darker masses at the center. If you looked closely you could see the suspension cartilage running from the implants to my rib cage. "I'd bet you have almost no weight on your breast skin at all," she said.

"You'd be right."

She nodded, but I got the impression she was hardly listening. She was too enthralled with my insides. She investigated my cardiovascular system, my nervous system, my bones and brain and blood. Last of all, she looked at my reproductive system, and I had to wonder why she didn't start there to begin with, because almost immediately she said, "Menopause."

"What about it?"

"That's what's happening to you. Your symptoms are pretty classic, though you don't have all of them." She frowned. "Didn't you say you'd been in a regeneration tank once?"

"Thirty-eight years ago." I gazed at the image of my ovaries and uterus on the monitor. They looked sort of like an elephant, with the fallopian tubes and the ovaries as the ears.

"Did you get the whole mess regrown then, or—?"

"Everything. I can't be going through menopause now, I should have another—"

"You are," she said firmly. "Count on it."

She was looking at the readouts on the right-hand side of the monitor screen and nodding to herself. Her certainty convinced me.

"Okay," I said. "Now what?"

She pulled a chair up and sat across from me, looking me directly in the face. She had been careful not to look at my naked body except in the line of duty, probably to put me at ease, which was almost funny. Being looked at naked was my greatest talent.

"I recommend regeneration. Starting immediately."

"How long will that take?" I said, and some of my horror must have crept into my voice.

"Six months," she said. "Longer if you take my advice and grow yourself some new skin, too. That youth padding stuff is very passé these days—are you all right?"

I had started to tremble. "I would prefer medication for now," I said. "Hormones or something, just to keep me going until—"

"If you opt for hormones your life span will never exceed one hundred," she said crisply. "Guaranteed. And your age will start showing pretty soon. You won't be youngish anymore."

"Well, maybe later I could—"

But she was shaking her head. "Lost ground is very hard to regain. This is a critical period in a woman's life, Lucy. You've got to seize the moment. We've made big strides in regeneration this last decade. You won't believe what we can do."

I rubbed my butch hair so hard my head went numb. She was looking at me with an implacable message in her eyes, like a parachute instructor getting ready to kick a frightened cadet out the door.

"You'll be safe here," she said. "This is the best possible way for you to go undercover. Believe me, I've been there. I know what you're up against."

"I lost my memory."

"What?"

"The first time," I said. "In regeneration. When I woke up, my past was gone. If I forget again, I'm a dead duck."

She was shaking her head again. "There's no earthly reason why you should have lost your memory. Extremely long-term regeneration can cause *temporary* memory loss, but never permanent."

"Thirty-eight years is not what I'd call temporary."

I got up and pulled my clothes on. I had expected her to argue with me, but when I turned back again, she was studying a file on the monitor. I was surprised to see my name on it.

"You had the Blue Clap," she said, as if sensing my stare.

"Yes."

"I wonder." She shut off the monitor and gazed at the floor, rubbing her lower lip.

"Yes?" I pulled on my shoes.

She looked up at me, still rubbing her lip. "I wonder if it got to your brain."

My stomach lurched. "They said no."

"They *said* no. They might have said it to spare you. I would, if I thought it was necessary for your emotional well-being. You were sixteen, right?"

"Yeah." I rubbed wet palms on my clothing. "Listen, I need to think about this. I need to sleep on it."

"Okay," she said compassionately. "Call me if you have any questions."

"I've got one right now."

"Yes?"

"How long have you been hiding out from Designer Gene Co.?"

Her face went blank, and she looked as if she would evade my question. But then she sighed and said, "For over a hundred years, Lucy. But don't ask me any more questions about that. It's not that I don't want to answer them, it's that you're in enough hot water as it is, just with Machine Co."

I nodded and started to leave. Before I could get through the door, she said, "Wait!"

I looked at her over my shoulder.

"Afterward, send him to me, okay?" She didn't look mad or jealous, just a little sad.

"I will," I promised, and went off in search of Joe.

*   *   *

I found him in the shower. The stall was transparent, obviously made for someone who was proud of his body. I sat down on the john and enjoyed the show while my feverish mind tried to balance cool thought with hot flashes. Joe lathered his beautiful olive skin and watched me out of the corner of his eye.

He turned off the water and dried himself with a big, soft purple towel. "You want a shower?" he asked.

"I'm about to take the longest bath of my life."

"Regeneration, huh? What for?" He stood with the towel at his side, not bothering to wrap it around himself. An erection tugged at his perfect loins as he listened to me talk about what Ann had said.

"You won't lose your memory, *querida*," he said. "Ann is the best doctor on Earth. She did me after Mars."

I nodded.

"I was going to suggest you hang around here a few months anyway. At least now you won't be bored."

He was right. Where was I going to go in the world with such big monsters after me? *Mykonos!* cried a little voice in my head, but it was just sad, wishful thinking.

"I'd like to watch you take a shower," he said.

I could probably have said no and he would still have kept me safe in his fortress. But I didn't say no.

He sat on the john and watched me while I lathered and scrubbed, paying special attention to points of interest. When I got out again, he had a full-blown erection. I had a moment of panic, thinking that if he kissed me when we were both naked, he wouldn't be able to resist wanting more. But he just handed me the towel and watched me dry myself.

"I never knew how nice it was to be watched until just now," he said, "when you watched me."

"I liked it," I admitted.

"I want to do something different this time. Don't worry, *querida*, I won't touch you. Not when you're feeling so bad."

The tone of his voice almost brought tears to my eyes again, but I fought them back. "What do you have in mind?"

"Come in here," he said. He managed to slide past me without touching me. I followed him into a comfortable-looking room with big, overstuffed chairs and shelves full of old-fashioned bound books. He pulled two chairs around until they were facing each other about six feet apart. "Sit down," he said. "I'll be right back."

He disappeared through another door and came back with a jar of oil. I had already caught on to what he wanted, and had positioned myself seductively in the chair. Lots of my clients had asked for this kind of thing. I was a master at it.

He sat in the other chair and poured oil into his palms. "You need any of this?" he asked me.

"No."

He began to stroke his penis with his oiled hands. "No," he said, his eyes burning with that strange spark as he looked at my body, "not you, Lucy. You have your own sweet juices."

I opened my legs to show him this was true and let my hands glide expertly over myself. My heart started to pound as I stroked my nipples, and the moment I touched my clitoris, my body tensed in unexpected delight. I had never performed with anyone in person before, and Joe was so beautiful. He didn't need any penile enhancement, his cock was large and curved slightly to the left. His left hand glided gently over the shaft while his right hand cupped and rubbed his balls. His hands were like the hands on Michelangelo's statue of David, veins standing out and pulsing with life.

I slid my hips forward and inserted two fingers inside my vagina, slipping them in and out with my hand turned slightly to one side so he could see what I was doing. My other hand touched and held my breasts as if it were his hand and not mine.

"I hate those fucking Machines," he said. "I've never slipped on one of those metal cunts. I always used my own hands. You know why, *querida?*"

"No."

"Because flesh on flesh is what I want. When I touch myself, I'm not just jacking off. I make love to myself. I love myself. I love you, Lucy."

My body started to tingle with heat that originated from deep inside my vagina. But I wasn't quite there yet. I wanted to make it last.

"Once you get used to metal on flesh, it's hard to go back," he said. "You lose your humanity."

I believed that. I know why I had needed my Machine all those years, and it sure as hell hadn't been for satisfaction.

My vagina was contracting and releasing around my fingers. I wondered what that looked like. Could he see what I felt? I had never looked into a mirror while having an orgasm. His face was my mirror. Yes, he could see it. His hands were tightening around his penis as he thrust his way to his own climax, and as I watched him, my whole body started to shake.

Joe cried out rhythmically, as his sperm shot out and over me, again and again. It was extremely impressive. He started to laugh.

"Jesus!" he said, and his laughter intensified his orgasm until it was all he could do to stay upright with his eyes open. When he finally wound down, my own was still going on, and I wondered if it would ever end. But finally my tremors subsided too, setting me down gently with a few delicious diminishing waves. He watched avidly, his hands resting on his still-hard penis.

"This is a new start for us, *querida*," he said. "I could be happy with this."

"Me too," I said, and was shocked at my own admission. But it was true. I hadn't enjoyed sex that way for a long, long time. If ever.

"While you're in the tank, I'm going to keep some feelers out with my Mars connections," he said, his eyes still traveling over my body with pleasure. My own were doing the same with his, loving his masculine angles. "You hear anything about the Ganymede war?"

"On the news net."

"The Martian government is thinking about backing the rebels. Against Earth, you know what I mean?"

"Jesus."

"Yeah. I'm trying to decide which side to come down on. I know a hell of a lot more about Earth defenses than Martian. So maybe I'll be a Martian this time."

My mind lingered over old images of a ruined Mars just after the war, cities destroyed and the very ground scarred and torn. Millions dead.

"There's this Greek island, Joe. My own paradise. I wanted to retire there."

"Maybe it'll still be there."

"Maybe it won't."

"Then I'll buy you another island, Lucy. You pick the one you want."

I was crying again; and as if on cue, my butt began to throb.

"Why do they have to have another damned war?" I cried.

"You mean those miners on Ganymede? Hell, I'd be doing the same thing if I were them. Just like in the Mars Revolt, *querida*. People get sick of being treated like slaves and seeing all their money go into someone else's pocket."

I didn't bring up the fact that in the Mars Revolt Joe had fought against the same people he was apparently sympathizing with now. I didn't need to. He certainly knew it.

"You're just feeling bad because of those old-lady ovaries you've got inside you," he said. "Once you've grown some young ones, you'll see things differently. I did. When I went in the tank after Mars, I was forty. When I came out, I was eighteen."

I nodded, but it all seemed unreal. I couldn't imagine ever feeling differently.

"Get some sleep, Lucy," he said. "That couch rolls out. Help yourself to the books or the news net." He got up and went to the outer door.

"Joe, Ann said—"

"I know." He blew me a kiss and walked out the door, still naked. I hoped Ann would like that.

In four weeks, the cultures Ann had harvested

from my body had grown into the pre-regeneration stage, and it was time to remove my skin. My reproductive organs, too, but the skin had me more worried. It wasn't like when I got the youth padding, when all they'd had to do was pull up the existing skin and pull it back down again. This was like something out of Francisco Goya's worst nightmare.

I stood naked in the empty regeneration tank while Ann and Joe cut my skin off. Joe had apparently helped her at it before, and once I got used to the idea I was actually kind of glad to have him there.

"Now I'm really gonna get under your skin, *querida*," he said. I was careful not to look at what they were doing; I felt nothing. Something in me wished that I would never get that sense back again.

I was dosed with good locals, but kept awake out of necessity as they removed my skin, strip by strip, and cut away the youth padding, replacing the whole mess with regenerating tissue and gradually filling the tank to keep it damp. The whole process took eight hours, not counting an hour and a half when Ann had to do the surgery in my abdomen and put the budding new organs in place.

She didn't plug in the sleep IV until I was in fluid up to my neck. "Having your face removed is traumatic," she said. "It's time to go to sleep."

"Good night," I said.

The last thing I was aware of was Ann and Joe floating over me in their sterile suits while I breathed in artificial amniotic fluid that I knew would turn me back into a young woman. They seemed to hover like angels, their hands caressing my face, which was turned upward for their blessings.

I could feel myself floating. *This is familiar*, I

thought to myself, and I flexed my hand to see if it was a fetus's hand. But I couldn't feel it at all, so I must have dreamed it.

Then nothing, for a long, long time. No more dreams, no thoughts, but possibly the barest awareness of existence, though it's hard to remember for sure. Perhaps I thought so later, because I couldn't imagine nonexistence, not even after the tank.

Eventually the light grew in my mind, and I opened my eyes. The tank was draining off the fluid, and I saw pale stuff floating around me like seaweed. I almost laughed when I realized it was my own hair. How long had I been in there, anyway?

The fluid drained below chin level, and I coughed it out of my lungs. My mind was alert, so at least I knew the oxygen had stayed at the proper levels.

Now let's see, I told myself. *My name is Lucy Cartier, I was a video prostitute for thirty-eight years, I lived at—* The process of listing memories was familiar, as if I had done that before, too. I went on and on with the list as the tank drained, absently admiring my new skin at the same time. It was pale and kind of grayish at the moment, but I had been warned to expect that. All of the seams had closed and I could feel my nerves coming to life, right on schedule.

Joe, my mind was thinking. *Mykonos, Machine Co., the war on Ganymede, Wendy's murder—* So far everything was there—at least it seemed so. The last of the fluid ran down the drain, and one side of the tank slid open, letting me out. I walked, slowly and awkwardly, but not without a feeling of having been rested, nurtured. My body felt strangely light, and my breasts didn't seem to tug at the new skin at all, almost as if they were still floating.

"Hello?" I called. "Ann?" I almost called Joe's name too, but stopped just in time. *Christ!* I thought. *Who knows who I'm going to find in here now?*

No one answered my calls. I walked around the lab and wondered if it was even the same lab. The equipment wasn't where it should have been, but it could have been rearranged during the months I was asleep. I went to the door and pushed the control buttons. It slid open.

Sunset-colored light poured through.

I went to a giant picture window, my body naked and cold, my wet hair plastered down my back all the way to my butt. I might have been in the tank for years, for all I knew. It didn't even matter how long I thought it was, because obviously something had happened to my memory after all. I stood in front of the window and gazed at a red landscape with a purple-blue sky.

I was on Mars.

"Hello, darling," said a voice behind me. I turned and found a pre-adolescent girl standing in the doorway of the lab, her body just barely beginning to blossom into womanhood. Her thick red hair hung in a long braid down her back, and she was wearing a cobalt bodysuit that might have been painted on, revealing every secret her little body could possibly have. I noted, absently, that she had no pubic hair.

Her face was lovely, elfin, with huge green eyes. She was smiling at me.

"Who are you?" I asked her.

Her smile widened.

"I'm your mother," she said. "Welcome home, Lysel."

She pronounced the name *LEE-zl*.

She and I sat at a breakfast of croissants and fruit on the terrace of her private suite, which overlooked a canyon system that dwarfed the one back in Arizona. The Valles Marineris was almost as long as North America was wide, and we were perched near the southern ridge of the central section, which is seven hundred kilometers at its widest. The northernmost ridge couldn't even be seen, it was so far away.

I was wearing a loose linen lounging suit over nice dry cotton panties and bra, which felt great after being wet for God knows how long. She was still wearing that cobalt thing, still looking like a child, but she certainly didn't talk like one, and I wasn't about to argue with her about anything.

"You were in the tank for two years," she said, between bites. She also had the hearty appetite of an adolescent. "There were some complications, but you've recovered from them."

"I feel fine," I said, for lack of anything better.

"You look like a girl again. I can't believe you wore that dreadful youth padding for so long! It was so primitive, and your face must have begun to show its age—" She shuddered fastidiously. "I've started you on nanones, dear. Now that you've been regenerated, you can get their full benefit."

"Nanones?"

"What do you think keeps me looking this way? I look eleven, right?"

She was sitting there with her long, coltish legs drawn up, their slender muscles firm and perfect in that pre-adolescent way no athlete could ever emulate. Her breasts were more a hint than a reality, yet her chest and shoulders curved in a heartbreakingly feminine fashion; the skin on her delicate face was as soft and dewy as the petals of a flower.

"Yes," I said.

"Well, I'm over three hundred."

I tried not to stare at her. Either it was an out-and-out lie or she was using Youth Technology that no one on Earth had ever heard of. No one at my income level, anyway.

"The trick is to get your body back to the pre-adolescent stage," she was saying. "Once you've done that, you can keep it that way indefinitely."

Back on Earth, I had thought Linda Tree made a pretty convincing nine-year-old, but she had been a petite woman with special alterations. She had used video techniques to give her skin the illusion of childishness. Eventually, she would have required skin regeneration—youth padding would have ruined the effect completely. But if she had been rich enough to afford Mother's alleged treatments—if people could take themselves back to that physical age—pedophilia would take on a whole new meaning . . .

My head was starting to spin, so I concentrated on

looking at the Valles M. It was so enormous, I didn't even get vertigo, because it was unreal.

And beautiful, so incredibly beautiful.

"I can't believe how beautiful your face is," she said, startling me. I looked at her again. She was regarding me with a clinical expression. It was the same expression Ann had worn during my examination, but it looked odd on her young face.

"Your body is about the same age it was when you left here," she said, "but you could be a different woman."

"Are you so sure I'm not?"

"Positive. Your genes are the same, dear. Let me see if I can guess what you've had done." She rested her delicate chin in her hand and looked me over. "The breasts and buttocks are obvious. And your legs were lengthened—how I wish I could have that done! But I have an allergic reaction to biometal. Anyway—your face."

She leaned closer and I resisted the urge to draw back. So far she had been pleasant, but she radiated about as much warmth as the ice in our glasses. "Your face has been marvelously sculpted. Who was your artist?"

"I designed it myself."

"Really! I'm glad to see you inherited some of my talent."

It was really too ludicrous. Her speaking mannerisms were adult, but her voice was high and girlish. She almost sounded like a young actress pretending to be old. I didn't discount that theory at all.

"Did I look like you—before—"

"Before you ran away?" she said brightly.

"I ran away?"

"You don't remember?"

"No. I would appreciate it if you could—"

"Of course, dear." She dabbed her lips with her napkin and sat back in her chair, drawing her legs up and sitting cross-legged. "Do you remember having the Blue Clap?"

"Yes."

"And do you remember who gave it to you?"

"No."

She cocked her head and gave me a soft smile.

"Truthfully, Lysel? You don't remember the boy you wanted to marry, the one you thought was the great love of your life?"

"No," I said, wondering what that little smile meant.

"I can't believe it. You've actually forgotten Joe Santos."

I was glad I wasn't eating or drinking at the moment, because I certainly would have choked. I think I managed to keep my face straight as I said, "Who?"

She laughed. "Well, your memory loss isn't a complete disaster, then. I hated that boy. He was the son of a laborer, for heaven's sake. He had looks, I'll give you that, but he must have fucked every girl in his worthless little town before he gave you that disease."

I took a casual sip of my iced coffee.

"I remember being a prostitute," I said. "Before the clap, I mean."

"Well, that's not a surprising delusion. You felt very dirty after being used by that boy. I remember you were inconsolable."

"And that's why I ran away?"

I thought her eyes narrowed, but I may have imagined it. "You suffered memory loss, Lysel. You were very disoriented. You became paranoid, convinced that people were after you, trying to kill you. I was told I should lock you in a hospital, but I thought that would be too cruel. You disappeared without a trace. I've been looking for you all these years."

"Why?"

She returned my gaze without blinking. "Because I love you," she said, in the same voice one might use to say, "My shoes are brown." She was utterly unconvincing, but maybe that didn't matter to her.

"I know you've been a prostitute all these years," she said.

"Yes." I was happy that at least some part of her story agreed with my own memories.

"I congratulate you for using a Machine in your work. You've avoided the worst aspects of your profession and made a good living. I have your paintings, by the way. I've put them in your quarters, you can arrange them as you see fit."

"Thank you, Mother," I said, but she didn't react to the word at all. I might as well have been calling her "Hey, you."

"Isn't my view fantastic?" she said, as she noticed my eyes wandering back to the canyon. "Look, a flier!"

I tried to see where she was pointing, but there was too much to snag my attention. Mother's complex was just a small part of the huge city built near the central section of Valles M., and I had to admit that whoever had designed the city had done so with considerable taste and ingenuity. Buildings blended perfectly with the canyons, not so much camouflaged as designed to complement. The sunset sky gave everything odd red and purple tones, and the only way I could tell that a weather dome was overhead was by the warm air that wafted across the terrace. The temperature might have been in the low eighties, and the air smelled of flowers and other plants, with a slight metallic aftertaste.

"There." Mother pointed a finger, and I suddenly caught sight of movement. Someone was hang-gliding over the central rift.

"You must do that while you're here," Mother was saying. "Our low gravity gives us many options you don't have on Earth. Not to mention that it's easier on the face and breasts." She didn't glance at my chest when she said that, so it sounded like a general comment.

"The air smells good," I said, when the silence had stretched past the bearing point. I hadn't meant the comment to mean anything much, but Mother laughed.

"You obviously don't remember your Martian past at all. No Martin ever compliments the atmosphere here. They crashed those asteroids about five hundred years back, and then they introduced those viruses—by the way, don't believe any tall tales about ethyl alcohol rain. We finally had to put in atmosphere plants about three hundred years ago."

"Oh."

She laughed again. "And then there are the dust storms. They cover the whole planet, some seasons. I'll let you watch one on our satellite screen; it's really quite a beautiful sight when seen with colored enhancements."

"I'd like that," I said, quite honestly.

She shrugged, a gesture that looked truly adolescent. "You'll like it the first few times. Then you'll get tired of it."

"You don't sound like you enjoy living here very much," I said.

She gave me a charming grin. "You're wrong. Mars is my place. She's just like me, an old broad made young again. Artificially, of course, but we're still working on it."

I wondered if she meant herself or the planet.

"Lysel," called a deep male voice, only this time it was pronounced Lee-SELL. A black man stepped onto the terrace. I mean a *black* man, his skin so dark it seemed to absorb all the light around him. I couldn't get a good look at him until he was a few feet away, and then there was much to admire.

He must have been six and a half feet tall, leanly muscled and perfectly proportioned. His hair was long, straight, and snow white, his eyes were almost gold. His features were African: a wide, full mouth, down-tilted nose with flared nostrils, and almond eyes. His white brows arched beautifully above his eyes, and he wore an oriental-style mustache, thin and long, hanging down below his clean jawline.

At first I thought he was naked, but then I saw he was wearing tights that were the same color as his skin.

"Child," he said, and pulled me out of my chair, right into his arms. "You've grown so beautiful." He hugged me just a little tighter than seemed appropriate, and his hands, when they released me, lingered just the least little bit.

"Lysel and I were watching a flier," said Mother. *LEE-zl* again. I thought she emphasized the word, but something else was bothering me just then.

He had touched me, and I didn't feel sick.

The next time the black man said my name, he was pronouncing it *LEE-zl*, like Mother. If he had stuck with his first pronunciation, I might not have been suspicious. "Do you remember me?" he asked. "I was your doctor."

"Rashad is the one who put you in the regeneration tank all those years ago," said Mother.

Rashad smiled at me with perfect white teeth. He looked nothing like the white doctor I remembered. Or thought I did.

"Did you know me when I was a child?" I asked him.

"I was a doctor in your mother's company." He sat gracefully in a chair between Mother and me, positioning himself so that the two of them seemed to be regarding me together, a unified front. "Designer Gene Co."

The people who were after Ann. My heart started to hammer in my chest.

"Designer Gene Co. is the company that created the Mars terraforming viruses I told you about earlier," Mother was saying. "I took over the company after it went bankrupt."

"Oh," I said and sipped more iced coffee.

"Don't you want to know what Designer Gene Co. does these days?" Mother asked, cocking her head in a way that I was beginning to realize meant danger.

"Yes. Did you say terraforming viruses? That's fascinating."

"Not anymore," said Mother. "That terraforming business is old news. We work on *people* now."

Rashad reclined in his chair, not so much to get

more comfortable as to show himself off. "We terra-form people," he said, smiling lazily.

"Don't be silly," Mother told him. "We're trying to find a way to replace regeneration, Lysel, and ultimately to make *rejuvenation* unnecessary."

I had heard talk of this sort of thing in the news net before. "Immortality?" I asked.

"Yes. Or something close to it. What we're really zeroing in on is the aging process. I suppose it's possible that a person could grow tired of living eventually, but we'd rather be able to choose our own time than have it thrust upon us."

"Have you grown tired of living?" I asked her.

She laughed. "My body thinks it's eleven years old! It wants to run, play, climb, eat—live! I'm convinced that this is the optimum age, the time when the human body is at its most perfect stage!"

For once I believed she was telling the truth. A fever was glowing in her eyes.

I glanced at Rashad to find him feasting his eyes on my implants. "I prefer a more mature stage," he said.

Mother shrugged, cool and bored again. "One could always have implants, if one desired. I don't care for them myself."

Another uncomfortable silence followed. For me, anyway. "Are you concerned about the birth and death rates?" I asked, finally. "The imbalance could cause trouble—"

"Immortality isn't for the masses," said Mother, with what looked like an honest sneer. "They can have the old Youth Technology. And the Machines that keep their birth rate down." She snickered. "And the diseases that keep the death rate up!"

"Sounds fair," I said, but the sarcasm seemed lost on her.

"Would you like to see your quarters?" she asked me. "Rashad and I have to go to work. Later I'll get together with you and we can talk about what you'd like to do here."

"Thank you," I said. "That sounds fine."

"Rashad, will you see Lysel to her suite? I'm going to freshen up and change." She was up and out of her chair before she had even finished speaking, and in another moment she was gone.

"I'd be happy to," said Rashad—to me, since Mother hadn't cared to wait for his answer.

"Your skin is petal-new," Rashad told me as we walked down a palatial hall toward my suite. "It is especially sensitive to UV rays right now, so you'll have to take extra precautions. Especially in our Martian atmosphere."

"Oh?"

"We have an ozone layer, and our weather dome filters out a lot of the harmful UV, but UV is one of the chief villains in the aging process. You should absorb as little of it as possible."

He had slipped into the same fastidious tone of voice Mother had used when speaking of aging. For the moment he was another Designer Gene doctor, clinical and obsessed.

"Is that why you made your skin so black?"

He laughed. "It's not black. Not exactly."

"What?"

He stopped and said, "Look. Watch the edge of my form as I turn in the light." He turned, and I watched.

I caught the vaguest sheen of color. "Purple?" I guessed.

"Yes," he was grinning as he looked at his own skin. "So dark, it looks blacker than black. Richer, too. I've patented the virus that causes it. You might want it yourself—you would look magnificent with this skin. You could keep your strawberry hair if you wanted."

"Maybe I'll take you up on that," I said, as much because I liked the idea of a disguise as for aesthetic considerations.

Pleased, he took my arm, and we continued down the hall. I didn't feel the slightest sickness at his touch, though his casual customs threw me mentally off balance. I wasn't sure what gestures were expected in return.

My shoes tapped on the tile, but his made no sound at all. Somehow I found that very disturbing.

"Has your skin always been dark?" I asked him, as we turned a corner and started down another long hall. Blue-purple light slanted in through beautiful, long windows that stretched almost to the twenty-foot ceiling.

"No!" he snorted. "It was brown. Boring, dull brown. I was constantly worried about UV, but now my eyes and my skin are perfectly protected."

"That's wonderful." So he wasn't white way back then. He wasn't the doctor from my fragmented memories.

"Here." He stopped in front of double doors that looked thick enough to block out a force blast. I couldn't tell if they were carved out of some extraordinarily strong wood or if they were paneled. Rashad keyed four numbers into an elegant pad near the lock, and one door popped open about an inch. He grabbed both handles and pulled the doors wide.

"Ah," he said, "here are your lovely paintings."

My art collection was propped against the walls and some packing crates. My eyes stung at the sight. But I refused to shed any tears. "Wonderful," I said lightly. "I'm going to enjoy arranging my rooms."

I had hoped that would be his cue to leave me alone, but instead he marched right into the living room and glared at the paintings, frowning fiercely, as if something were missing or damaged. I had seen his expression on the faces of certain kinds of people at museums, so I ignored him and explored my suite.

There was a small kitchen, a dining area, a large living room, a room that might serve as an office, a bedroom, and a bathroom. I found a vidphone in the bedroom, but no monitors for news or entertainment nets.

The bedroom was my favorite room. It had a huge picture window on one wall and a terrace like Mother's on another, both giving me a breathtaking look at the Valles M. More hang gliders were floating over the central rift. The scene was so huge, I found myself thinking of Mars as gigantic, dwarfing Earth. But as I recalled, it was only about half the size of Earth, and the gravity was substantially less. If I hadn't spent the last two years floating in fluid, I might have been more aware of that.

I turned and found Rashad in the doorway, staring at me. His expression wasn't clinical anymore. "You're incredible," he said. "Once your skin regains its normal color, you'll look even better."

"How long will that take?" I asked, trying to keep the conversation businesslike.

"A week or so," he said, his eyes on my breasts. He was beautiful, but I wanted him to get out of my room and leave me alone.

"I'd like some quiet time now, if you don't mind," I said. "I'm still getting used to things."

I had thought he would be stubborn, but instead he backed off immediately. He looked a little miffed. "I've got work to do," he said and marched out of the room. I heard the front doors slamming behind him.

I went out onto my terrace and sat in a large padded lawn chair. I took several deep breaths, using the yoga training I thought I remembered, and then I took inventory of other memories.

Joe and Ann were clear in my mind, as if I had just spoken to them the day before. I could see them floating with me in the tank. I could see Joe sitting in the chair across from me, stroking his beautiful penis, looking at me with hot eyes. I could see the sympathy in Ann's eyes as she told me I'd have to go into regeneration.

I could see Wendy the hermaphrodite, mutilated on her Machine. I couldn't bear to think of Ann and Joe that way.

Mother's story of my past was an interesting one. She had planted doubt in my mind concerning Machine Co.'s plot to kill me. Not much doubt, but I could see where paranoia could have shaped my memories. It would have helped if I could have remembered how I came to Earth—assuming I wasn't already there—and what had happened soon thereafter.

My earliest memory was of that white doctor. I concentrated on him. There he was, calling me "Miss

Cartier," telling me I might not survive the Blue Clap. He was bending over my bed, struggling to conceal the horror and pity he felt. He was tall, thin, about thirty, watery blue eyes, with thinning sandy hair . . .

That was odd. No one had thinning hair, even forty years ago. There were dozens of ways to regenerate hair, change its thickness, texture, color. They'd been doing that for centuries, and *no one* had thinning hair these days. So why did he have it?

Maybe because the memory was false. Maybe because my whole life was false.

I left the terrace and went into the bathroom, stripping my clothes off as I went. One wall was mirrored. I stood in front of it and studied myself. My skin was extremely pale and had a slightly gray pallor; but it looked young. I looked young. I looked no more than sixteen, except, of course, that my breasts and my butt didn't quite fit the image. I looked like a fantasy girl, like an image out of a wet dream, much more so than I ever had as a video prostitute.

I looked hard, turned up the lights as bright as they would go, but I couldn't find a line, wrinkle, or sagging spot anywhere. And what's more, I *felt* young. I could relate to what Mother had said about her body, whether she was telling the truth about her age or not. Judging from the image in my mirror, she was.

A three-hundred-year-old girl. It was staggering.

Was she watching me now, she and Rashad? I didn't much care. I didn't bother to get dressed again as I went into my living room and feasted my eyes on my art collection. I had thought I would never see it again. Arranging it would keep me busy, keep me from wondering what was going to be done to me and why I was even alive to begin with. Or if Mother was really my mother or my jailer.

And what about Scorpianne? asked the inner voice that seemed to love to torment me.

"What about her?" I wondered back, annoyed. Scorpianne was back on Earth, a problem left far behind.

Are you sure? That thought slipped in like a thief, but once acknowledged, it didn't seem inclined to go away again. All I knew about Scorpianne was that she was probably a woman. I didn't know what she looked like; for all I knew, Mother could be Scorpianne. Lord knows, she scared me almost as much.

It occurred to me that there was one simple way to see if I was simply feeling paranoid out of habit. I went to the door and tried to turn the handle.

It was locked.

I shrugged and went back to arranging my collection.

◀◀ ❚'m sorry, dear," Mother said. "Rashad didn't re-
❚alize the door locks automatically when it's shut.
❚And he was in such a hurry he forgot to give
you the code."

She had awakened me at 8:00 a.m., looming over
my bed with her curly red hair down about her
shoulders, looking like the Faerie Queen from one
of those decadent paintings from the late nineteenth
century. She hardly looked like an assassin then, like
someone who might call herself "Scorpianne."

"Why didn't you come for dinner last night?" she
had asked me, and I told her about the locked door.
When she smiled, I thought there was a touch of
malice at the corners of her mouth and her eyes
seemed too bright. But the light in my room was so
dim, and she hardly seemed real. How could she
harm me?

Mother gave me a tour of the residential floor,
making sure I knew where the kitchen and the gym
were. "We always serve ourselves here," she told
me. "And no one has the same schedule, so don't
worry about getting up at any particular time."

But when we went out to her terrace, breakfast
was waiting, and somehow I got the impression

Mother hadn't set it there herself. Maybe the doctors were Mother's servants, when she wanted it that way.

She ate twice as much as me, stuffing muffins, fruit, and scrambled eggs into her mouth at an alarming rate, yet still managing to look delicate as she did so. Her little body just seemed to absorb it all—her stomach didn't even bloat. That raised questions in my mind about metabolism and its effect on the aging process, but I saved them, for the time being.

"I know this is all very difficult for you," she said, when she was done with the muffins. "It must have seemed like you were kidnapped, but that wasn't the case at all. I simply couldn't leave you to the primitive regeneration techniques on Earth, not with the cutting-edge technology I have at my disposal."

"You worked on me?" I pretended to be too busy with a banana to look at her.

"Yes. The skin regeneration was already well progressed by the time my agents found you, but I used nanones to make certain other changes. Or you could call them viruses, if that seems more familiar. Your whole system has been overhauled, dear. Now you don't just *look* young, you *are* young."

I felt it, too. I was alert, full of energy. I didn't have the usual aches and pains I had grown so used to having in the morning. "My doctor put in new ovaries and a uterus," I said.

"He did a decent job of that." She frowned as she worked the peel off of a red citrus fruit. "But he was odd. Did you notice his hairline? Why would anyone let his hair go thin in this day and age?"

"I don't know," I said. "Maybe he was absent-minded."

She laughed at that. "Anyway, I have some fun stuff planned for today. I thought you'd like to shop for some new clothes and see a little of New Barsoom."

"New Barsoom?"

"The old one was destroyed in the Mars Revolt."

Apparently she was talking about the city. I wondered if I would learn her name in the same matter-of-fact fashion.

"We won't try to see *too* much today," she was saying. "The whole thing is just too big. Though we can fly over the central rift if you would like."

"On hang gliders?"

"No!" she laughed like a child. "In an aircraft. We'll save the gliders for a braver day."

That seemed sensible, though the idea really hadn't frightened me. Perhaps the reality of the situation hadn't penetrated.

"I have my own favorite shops," she said, indicating the light blue bodysuit she was wearing. "As you can see, most of us here prefer comfortable clothes that let us move. If that's what you like, we'll go to Lorilei's and Dream Stuff."

"I like this jumpsuit," I said. It was the same one I had worn the day before, and I liked the way it looked.

"That's a work coverall," she said, smirking at me.

"I like linen," I said, unruffled. "Also silk blends, cotton blends, rayon—"

"Don't worry. Any fabric you can think of, synthetic, organic, or engineered, can be found in Martian shops. You won't be disappointed."

*   *   *

I expected a heavy security gate outside Mother's complex, but there was none. In fact, I saw no security system at all, anywhere inside or outside of the building. Somehow that didn't comfort me. It only lent the situation a dreamlike quality, an illusion of safety that didn't fool my subconscious. A smaller sun than the one I was accustomed to was climbing straight up in the purple-blue sky—all the scene lacked was some melting clocks to make it one of Salvador Dali's paintings.

Mother had a private vehicle, which she drove herself, down magnificent, cobalt-colored roads. "Pig iron," she explained to me. "Some of the early atmosphere viruses released the oxygen from the iron oxide. They also shit pig iron, which became so plentiful—" she gestured around us.

If the roads were iron, the glass was certainly diamond. I'd seen windows like that in fancier parts of Phoenix, and their beauty was unmistakable. But even the commonest buildings in this resort town had diamond glass—some of them seemed to be at least 90 percent constructed of it. Shops, offices, hotels, housing complexes, restaurants—the least of them would have put the best of Phoenix to shame. There were even men with blowers cleaning the sidewalks.

But those weren't blowers. A second look told me that they were *vacuuming*—and not just the sidewalks. Every surface was being fastidiously vacuumed. When our vehicle had passed, they cleaned the road behind us. I wondered if the dust problem was really that bad.

"What do you think of the people?" Mother asked

me. Her tone wasn't exactly light. I decided the question was more complicated than it seemed.

"I've noticed how young everyone looks," I said. "And how attractive."

"They're not just attractive," said Mother. "They're great-looking, beautiful, handsome, whatever you want to call it. We insist on it."

Even the guys operating the vacuums were great-looking. "What do you need to get in here?" I joked. "A modeling license?"

"That's not far from the truth," she said. She parked her vehicle in front of some exclusive shops and jumped out. I followed her. I always seemed to be at least half a pace behind her, which might have been deliberate on her part or might have been because she was eleven and had more energy than I did. We walked past some of those vacuuming men and some other workers, all of whom had distinctive coveralls rather like the thing I was wearing. They looked us both over without apparent fear of reprimand. Mother smiled at them, like a flirting child.

"We don't pay our workers that much," she said, not seeming to care who heard her. "But we reward them with Youth Technology."

"I thought you said that wasn't for the masses."

"Not the cutting edge, dear. But we can give them better than you had on Earth. The only company as close to the cutting edge as we are is YoungTech in the orbital colony . . ."

She yanked open a door and swept us both into a shop. Immediately three clerks greeted us in a reserved but properly deferential fashion. Mother waved them off, and they melted into the background.

"I'm sure you know your way around a fine shop,

Lysel," said Mother. "Look around and see what you like. I have an unlimited line of credit here."

I was sure she did. She apparently intended to do some shopping herself, so I allowed myself to study the clerks as much as I did the clothing.

They weren't just youngish. They were *young*. Yet they had a polish, a glint to their eyes that betrayed their maturity.

Mother disappeared into another room.

"May I ask your assistance?" I addressed a girl who had noticed me looking around and had discreetly approached me.

"What can I do?" she said, her eyes busy trying to look me over without being disrespectful. She had the barest hint of an accent, one I couldn't place. Martian, I supposed; though Mother and Rashad didn't have one. They both spoke exactly like System newscasters.

"I'm new here," I said. "I'll need some undergarments—"

"We have Adoni, Willa, Softouch . . ."

"I love Softouch bras."

"This way—"

She led me into the third room, placing even more space between Mother and me. I kept an eye on the door while I probed. It was easy to pick out the things I needed, but I wanted the clerk to believe I needed her.

"This cotton feels so good against my skin," I chatted as I picked up a double-E peach underwire. "I was in regeneration so long, I thought I'd never get dry again."

"You look great!"

"Thank you." I picked ten bras in various colors,

knowing I only wanted five of them. "Will you help me out in the dressing room?"

She gave advice and offered her opinion as I tried on each one. I stripped completely naked to give her the full impact, then watched her while she examined me. She did it so gracefully, I knew I was dealing with an older woman. Her interest seemed to be personal, but not romantic.

"Were you born with that face?" she asked finally.

"No. It's sculpted."

"Really? Who was your artist?"

I smiled modestly. "I designed it myself."

Her eyes lit up. "It's exquisite! Do you do it professionally?"

I had been trying to get her to talk about her own youth treatments, but this was going in an interesting new direction.

"Yes," I lied. "Back on Earth. I thought it was high time I came to where the real action is, though. Earth is behind the times."

"I know." She handed me the lilac lace bra. "I hear they're still doing youth padding back there."

"They're beginning to shift to skin regeneration," I said, though I could tell she really wanted to get back to the face sculpting.

"Do you have a business card?" she asked me.

"No, but I'll have them soon."

"I'd love to have you do my face." She said that casually, but I could hear the undercurrent, that same obsessive quality I had heard in Rashad's tone. I looked at her.

"What do you think?" she asked hopefully. She was very pretty already—Hispanic, though her hair and brows were auburn, possibly implanted. The brows were nicely shaped but too thin. Her eyes were almost perfect.

"With a few subtle changes, you would outshine any woman in the room," I said.

"Except for you," she accused, but she sounded pleased. "Where are you going to set up shop?"

"I'm not sure yet."

"I usually go to Upscale. I had regeneration there last year."

"Upscale?"

"They do good work," she said, "but you might be too good for them."

She was hinting there, trying to get a price. I decided to risk a personal question.

"How old are you?"

"Thirty-five," she said.

"You look twenty." She really did.

"How old are you?" she asked back, since I had asked first.

"Fifty-six."

"God!" Her composure slipped a little. "You look seventeen."

I shrugged and faked another smile. "I'll come back when I've got my setup and give you a card. Can you show me some matching underwear?"

She was so happy that I had agreed to consider doing her, I think she would have stripped right there and given me her own underwear if I had asked.

By noon, Mother's vehicle was loaded down with our purchases and we were both starved, so we had lunch at one of the outdoor cafes. I looked at the faces and forms of the people at the surrounding tables, but this time with a different perspective. I wondered how they could be improved.

"I think I know what I want to do here, Mother," I said.

"What?" she inquired between bites of sesame barbecue chicken on Martian rye.

"I want to be an artist."

"You want to paint?"

I was surprised, since she was the one who had asked me which *artist* had designed my face.

"No. Facial design."

Her eyes got wide, which was rather hard to interpret. She might have been surprised or she might have been upset. But she said, "Of *course*! That's *perfect*! Your own face proves you can do it. I'll set you up in an office immediately."

"I'd like to work in town—"

She waved that away impatiently. "You don't want to work on the poor people. You should do top clients."

"How do you define poor?"

"People who can't afford a million dollars for a design."

"Are you joking?"

She gave me a mischievous smile. But she said, "No."

I had paid fifty thousand for my facial restructuring, and I had demanded the best. I had saved money by doing my own design—otherwise it would have been seventy-five thousand. I took a few contemplative bites of my Martian beef on orbital sourdough before answering her. Despite myself, I was excited. I may have wasted too many years as a prostitute. Perhaps I really was finding my true vocation.

Assuming I was going to live much longer.

"I would rather practice on the poor," I said at last, "before working on the rich."

"Well, that's a good point," she said. "Maybe a town office would work out in the beginning. But I'd like you to work with Designer Gene doctors. You may as well get accustomed to them right away." She raised an eyebrow at me. "Unless you'd rather work for another company? YoungTech, perhaps?"

That wasn't as neutral a question as it seemed. "No, Mother. I want to work with the best."

She nodded, then glanced over my shoulder. "Turn around," she said. "I want you to have a look at these two."

I turned and immediately knew who she was talking about. A man and a woman were walking through the tables, either arriving or leaving. He was the same color as Rashad, though he had opted for red hair instead of white. She had extremely long black hair and skin the color of jade.

Everyone looked at them openly, a change from the discreet glances the beautiful people had been giving each other. He was taller than Rashad, well muscled, but with features that suggested the Mongolian. Her features were Chinese, though the absence of an epicanthic fold on her lids marred the otherwise perfect presentation. She was willowy, tall, and pubescent, almost as young-looking as Mother. She affected not to notice the stares, but when her path brought her directly into Mother's line of sight, she glanced over.

Her eyes were as green as her skin. They went wide in fear.

I glanced at Mother. She was wearing the exquisite

smile she had worn the day she had met me coming out of the tank.

The couple continued on and left the cafe. Mother went back to her sandwich. "Those two will be on your client list," she said. "They're perfection junkies."

"Million-dollar junkies, you mean?"

"*Billion*-dollar. Our viruses don't come cheap. But we're already introducing cheaper, short-term pigment viruses for the workers. It's the new thing."

She was telling the truth about that; I could hear people excitedly discussing their skin at the surrounding tables. I saw plenty of people with the brown or gold skin you could get from melanin enhancers, not to mention pale-skinned people using inhibitors; but that was primitive. Within a year, rainbow-colored people would inhabit the resorts of Mars.

I couldn't help but smile as my eyes drifted from table to table, sizing up the *poor* people. The *workers*. Mother was a liar if she was claiming they didn't make her rich, couldn't make *me* rich. I was getting plenty of return looks of the sort the clerk at the shop had given me. Finally, my gaze lit on a man in a military uniform, sitting just two tables away, and my heart lurched in my chest.

I thought I was looking at Joe.

I immediately averted my eyes until I could get my heart rate down again. I tried to eat and drink without looking rushed or strained. Mother was eating more Martian red citrus with gusto, her bright eyes sliding idly—or seemingly so—over people and things.

I glanced back at the man. He smiled at me, and

that immediately told me he wasn't Joe. I remembered Joe's smile, aggressive, inviting, perhaps a little insane.

This man's smile was shy. He could have been Joe's brother, but his eyes were different too. They didn't have the electricity. It was spooky, though—he was wearing a military uniform.

"He's handsome," Mother said.

"What service is he with?" I asked, as if that were all I cared about.

"Space-air," she said. "Probably one of the fighter pilots."

I smiled back at him, partly because I wanted to and partly because I wanted Mother to think I was just flirting.

"Do you want me to find out who he is?" she asked.

"No," I said. "I'm still getting used to being . . ."

"It won't take you long, dear." She leaned back, dabbing her mouth with a napkin, and cocked her head. "Unless you have sexual hangups. You're not the guilty type, are you?"

"No."

"That would be fatal for a prostitute, I should think."

She didn't seem concerned that people might hear her saying that. I wondered if she thought I was concerned.

The man was still looking, and I looked back. I couldn't help myself. Could he be Joe, demonstrating acting abilities that put mine to shame? Whoever he was, I let him know I liked him.

He blushed under his olive complexion.

"He should be interesting," said Mother.

I nodded, my head beginning to spin with the effort of controlling my expression.

After lunch we headed straight for the flitter port. "Flitters are the best way to see the canyons," Mother explained. "They're small and expensive to ride. Most people have to take the train that goes *around*."

Around. That would be like going from Oregon to North Carolina.

"Why aren't there any bridges?" I asked.

"That would be an *enormous* job," said Mother, throwing her arms wide. The wind was getting stronger as we walked across the pig-iron lot toward the main gate. I had to fight to keep my new dress from blowing up to waist level. My hair mingled with Mother's in the air.

"But not impossible," I mused.

"Quite impossible. The rock around the edges of the canyons is crumbly. We have landslides all the time. We lose enough structures as it is—"

"Ladies—!" Someone was calling, with the same accent the shopgirl had used, only much more pronounced.

We turned and saw the Joe look-alike approaching with two other uniformed men. He had left the cafe just before we did, and my surprise at seeing him again lasted only a moment.

"Excuse us," he said, with that shy smile. "I'm Captain Morales. May I ask if you were intending to take a flitter across the canyon system?"

Mother smiled radiantly. "Yes . . ."

I was distracted for a moment by Captain Morales's men. They were the first people I'd seen in New Barsoom who weren't *great-looking*. They were

young, trim, well-built; their skin was clear and un-
blemished, their cropped hair was thick. But they
were ordinary; unlike their handsome captain, who
was saying, "We're scheduled to make a survey
flight in fifteen minutes. We get a much more spectacular look at the canyon system in one of our helicraft than you'd get in a flitter. Would you like to
come along with us?"

"Is there room for us in your craft?" Mother
teased. Her body looked naked in the afternoon light,
as if her bodysuit were painted on, and the men became flustered as they experienced her full attention.

"Plenty of room." Captain Morales glanced at me.

"What do you think, Lysel?" Mother asked.

"I'd like to get a good look at the canyon."

Morales and his men grinned.

The military port diminished behind us as we
moved out over the rift in our VIP passenger vehicle.
There were plenty of seats for civilians, but Captain
Morales had steered me into an observation dome at
the rear.

"The view is better here," he told me, but the seat-
ing was cramped. We had to squeeze together.

Mother was sitting up front with two lieutenants
and a couple of airmen, all of whom were vying for
her attention—when they weren't busy piloting the
craft, that is.

"Is that another military installation?" I asked Morales, indicating a huge structure that was coming up
on our left, dwarfing the surrounding buildings. It
had its own airfield, with flitters taking off and
landing.

"Yes," he said, his breath warming my ear. "We

like to maintain a visible presence all over Mars. It makes people feel safer."

I nodded as if I understood perfectly, but I was really thinking that I couldn't believe it was me sitting so close to another human being. Especially him. His body felt hard and smooth, and I was surprised at how good it smelled. I could smell his breath, too, sort of a blend of mint, food, and sex. His face was very close to mine, and his eyes said a lot more than his voice did. I felt giddy, like a much younger girl out on her first date. As far as I knew, it *was* my first date.

For a long time we were quiet, just watching the red gulfs beneath us. I knew we must be traveling very fast, but the Valles M. was so huge that we might have been suspended in space, hardly moving at all.

We could hear Mother through the intercom.

"What's your name, sweetheart?" a lieutenant asked her.

" 'Sweetheart' will do," she said, brushing her fingertips over his face and smiling like an angel.

"Come on, baby," he said seductively, obviously thinking he was talking to a young girl. "Mine's Jeff. What's yours?"

She cocked her head, charming him. "Call me Master," she said.

"Yes, Master," he laughed.

Morales turned the intercom off.

I felt his fingers brushing my shoulder, then his hand settling there, sliding appreciatively over bone and muscle and finally holding me. I shifted my weight so that I was leaning into him.

In the distance, a metal giant was grinding its arms

into the ground. Huge tubes stretched behind it, seeming to go right up into the atmosphere.

"Mining installation," Morales told me.

"You don't mine your satellites?"

"That too. Mars has a low gravity well, so we can use mass drivers to get the ore up to the orbital refineries. They take it straight to Earth."

He sounded a little bitter when he said *Earth*.

"Certainly not *all* the ore," I said. "Your need for raw materials must be huge. The atmosphere plants alone would use up—" I broke off when I realized he wasn't really listening. He was too busy feasting his eyes on me.

"Captain—" I said.

"Rico." His accent was almost Southwestern, like the one Joe had when he was feeling relaxed. Maybe some parts of Mars had been colonized by Hispanics. I had never bothered to wonder about that before.

"Rico, do you know who my friend is?" I nodded in Mother's general direction.

"No. Should I?" He was less shy now that he was getting used to me, but the vein in his neck was pulsing feverishly.

"She owns Designer Gene Co."

His face shifted subtly with comprehension. It was another thing he shared with Joe. He studied my face from chin to crown. "And who are you?" he asked, his voice low.

"I'm her daughter," I whispered.

The look of disbelief on his face told me something. "Are you new on Mars?" I asked him.

"I grew up in Tharsis City. That's another Mars completely."

"Not a lot of Youth Technology in your town, huh?"

"Not like *that*." He stared at the rest of my body openly, yet still managed to seem shy. "So you're a fancy girl, huh? I should have known. No one could be as beautiful as you are and be natural."

"Tell me something." I put my hand on his thigh and leaned farther into him. We were in the same position we would use if we were going to kiss. He was taking short breaths through his mouth now. "Do you know me?" I asked him.

"I do now."

"So you've never seen me before today?"

"I would remember if I had, baby."

"You're not working for Mother, then."

His brows drew together like thunderclouds. "As far as I know, I work only for the space-air force."

"How old are you?" I asked.

"Twenty-five."

I looked at his skin. He could have been turning twenty-five—for the first time. And it wasn't Joe's skin I was looking at, I was sure of it. Even the tension of the muscles underneath was subtly different. I found myself wanting to taste it.

"So, Lysel," he said, "you like to slum?"

"My name isn't Lysel. It's Lucy."

"I thought she called you— "

"She did."

His eyes lingered on my mouth. "Rich people are crazy," he told my lips.

"Crazier than you can imagine. Can I be honest with you?"

He didn't answer, but I told him anyway. "I was a video prostitute before I came to Mars."

"With one of those Machines?" he asked, his tone somewhere between arousal and disapproval.

"Yes."

"We don't use those much here. Not anymore."

"*What?*" Now it was my turn to be shocked.

"Who wants to fuck a Machine when beautiful women like you are walking around?"

It was so much like what Joe had said to me, a shiver went up my spine.

"Are you cold, baby?" His hand tightened on my shoulder. His touch wasn't like Rashad's at all. It made my heart pound. "Are you still in the business?" he asked.

Not even for your Joselito?

"No. I design faces now."

He lifted my chin with his fingertips. "You're one of those phonies, aren't you? This face isn't yours."

"No, it isn't."

"I don't care."

He kissed me, tired of waiting for my permission. My head exploded with memories of Joe's mouth. How I had feared this moment, the way he could draw it out so long, how he could seem to probe me all the way to my most vulnerable center. But now the memory made me so excited I felt faint. Rico's mouth was different, gentler, and his hands touched my breasts like he was afraid they would bruise. But I was kissing Joe too, in my fantasies. Finally enjoying him the way I had always secretly wished I could.

Rico pulled away and dabbed at my face with his fingers. "Why are you crying?"

"Just emotional."

"I want to see you again."

"You will," I promised. "How can I get in touch with you?"

His brows threatened another storm. "You don't want me coming to your home?"

"I don't want you to get killed."

He ducked down slightly to get a look at Mother. I could hear her girlish laughter and the laughter of the men.

"Does she have ideas about who you should and shouldn't date?" he whispered.

The question was almost touching.

"Frankly, I don't know. I never met the woman until yesterday."

"You never met your own mother?"

"If that's what she is."

He let out a long breath. "You're confusing me, Lucy."

"I have a damaged memory, Rico. I need to see you because you look like someone I knew—think I knew. But I want you to understand that the little girl flirting with your men up there is deadly, whether she's my mother or not. She's also got some funny ideas about *poor* people. You know what I mean?"

"I know what you mean." His face hardened, though it had yet to meet Joe's rigidity standards. "So, this guy you knew. I really look like him?"

"Exactly," I whispered.

"Did you like him a lot?"

"I loved him."

"I hope I can live up to his memory," said Rico, and he kissed me again.

I dreamed that we were swooping above the Valles M., but it was Joe who sat with me in the observation dome. *Look at it*, querida. His mouth was moist and warm next to my ear. *It looks like you could hide a whole planet in there.*

The helicraft tilted crazily above the central rift, and down we went. The dream-colored sky turned the rocks purple and blue where they might have been white as their bones were exposed by red land-slides. *I have you, baby*, said Joe, when he saw I was afraid. The floor of the canyon was miles away, and it seemed I could see every inch of it, all the way to the bottom.

"You never call me 'baby,'" I said. "You call me '*querida*.'"

Who do you think I am? he whispered. *Don't you know me when you see me?*

I looked, and now he was Rico. *You want me to die for you, baby?* he asked.

"No!"

I would, he promised. *I will.*

"Who are you, really?"

You think I'm working with her? Or maybe she told you the truth when she said I gave you that disease all those years ago. Or maybe I'm dead.

The helicraft turned upside down, an impossibility.

"Make it stop, Joe!" I pleaded.

Sorry, querida, he said. *This is how it's gonna be from now on.*

In the morning, Mother wanted to have breakfast with me again. She seemed fresh, cheerful, enthusiastic about my new career.

"You're going to make a lot of money for this company, Lysel," she said.

I watched her spoon oatmeal with bananas and

peaches into her mouth for a few moments, then asked her, "Mother, what's your name? I don't remember it."

Mother chewed for a moment, without looking up, then said, "Ann."

She smiled slowly, the corners of her mouth stretching as far as they could across her little face before she finally raised her eyes to mine. They twinkled at me, mischievously. She cocked her head and said, "What difference does it make what my name is, Lysel? You're going to call me Mother, aren't you?"

"If that's what you want," I kept my eyes level with hers and blank.

"That's what I want," she said. "And I always get what I want."

"Yes, Mother," I said, and finished my coffee.

heard Scorpianne's footsteps late one night. I was sitting in my living room, going over some client videos, taking notes and actually enjoying myself, when the sound came through my double doors.

CLUNK, CLUNK, CLUNK, CLUNK—

The same footsteps I had heard outside my old apartment, back on Earth. They were coming down the hall, toward my suite, slowly, as if the feet that made the sound were at the end of some very long legs. In fact, as if they weren't *feet* at all, but something hard and huge. Did she use a robot when she killed, and was it the same sort she used when she raped? Was it Mother, sitting in her room with her remote control, smiling that childish, beautiful smile while she played killer? I felt an abstract curiosity, but no panic at all.

CLUNK, CLUNK, CLUNK, CLUNK—

So I was going to die after all. I had actually forgotten to be afraid of Scorpianne since I had awakened, and now I could only wonder why she had waited so long. What purpose had I served that I was now done with? If only I could ask for the truth before I died. If she was really Mother, I could ask. Mother would know the answers. Mother probably knew more than I wanted her to tell me.

But the sound went past my door—CLUNK, CLUNK, CLUNK, CLUNK—and faded away down the hall.

I opened the door and peeked. Mars has no moonlight, so I had to strain to see anything in the starlight. Nothing moved. I closed the door again and locked it. But I wasn't afraid anymore, not of the footsteps.

Maybe Rico had told me something important when he had said he didn't like Machines. Mars was another planet altogether. Did Machine Co. even have an office here? I went to my terminal and called up a business directory. I didn't have an outside line, but at least I could find out who did business here.

There was no listing for Machine Co.

I felt a moment of elation; but then Scorpianne's voice seemed to speak in my ear, distorted slightly by the voice mechanism of her rape Machine. I could remember her exact words: *I've received checks from them. From someone else too, someone you don't remember.*

Mother. My assassin or my malignant savior.

I couldn't imagine what she wanted with me. But I would find out sooner or later. I didn't doubt that in the least.

In the morning, I met with the clerk from the clothing store, in my new office, downtown. Her name was Bette Rodriguez.

"You don't have a receptionist?" she asked when she wandered in from the outer office.

I shrugged. "I like to communicate with my clients in person, without a middleman." And I didn't want one of Mother's spies to deal with, either. Assuming Mother had spies, or even needed them.

I did have a Designer Gene Co. doctor, though, a fellow I liaisoned with in the evenings. Later he would get together with both me and my clients, and we would all discuss possibilities.

"You'll like Doctor Hasagawa," I told Bette. "He does exceptional work."

"I'm so excited," she said, though she seemed to be suppressing that emotion from her voice. "I can't believe I'm getting a Designer Gene team for just one hundred thousand."

Fifty for me and fifty for the doc. When I told him the price, he just shrugged his elegant shoulders.

"Well, let's get started." I directed her to a chair next to my monitor and dialed her three-dimensional image up on the screen. The resolution was so good that Bette almost seemed to be in two places at once. "Here are the changes I'd like to suggest," I said. "I'm going to give you a poster printout at the end of the session so you can take it home and really think about it. But first, tell me honestly: have you ever had facial surgery before?"

"Just brow implants," she said, gazing at her image as if it were a fascinating diagram. "I got those when I got my new hair."

"Eye tattooing or sculpting?"

"No," she said, and she seemed to mean it.

"Nose job?"

"Does a bump removal count?"

"Yes," I said, and sighed inwardly. If it was the sort of bump I suspected, I would have to amend my proposed changes. Some people hated any hint of ethnicity in their faces, and somehow the nose always turned out to be the biggest villain in their list of self-hating nitpicks.

"I want to warn you that I believe in subtlety," I said. "Your new face will look different from different angles, and I want all of them to be beautiful."

"Me too," she agreed.

So I showed her. I wanted to thicken the brows while retaining their nice shape. I *had* wanted to add a slight bump to her nose, one that would have given her back some of the exquisite ethnicity she lacked; but instead I asked her what she liked and disliked about her nose. She said she thought it was perfect—rather warningly, I thought; so I left it alone.

"Now, these slight changes to your lips, chin, and cheeks will produce *this* effect," I said, and I turned the image back and forth so she could see it from all angles.

She gasped in delight. "I never would have thought of that!"

"Your ears are perfect, in my opinion," I went on. "I hope you don't want to change them . . ."

"My ears? I never even notice them. Listen, do you think a beauty mark would fit in with this picture?"

"Sure. Here."

I put one on the right side of her face, emphasizing her new cheekbone while also lending her nose the little extra panache I thought it needed. The effect was really lovely.

"I've always wanted one of those!" she said. "I'll write you a check."

She was already sold, but I knew the bigger clients would feel more like I had. They would want to move carefully. But I was glad she was happy, anyway.

Later I met with Hasagawa, on my terrace. I almost smiled when I remembered I had told Bette she'd like Doctor Hasagawa. It had been one of those silly pleasantries, meaning that his work was superb, not that he was a nice guy.

He never seemed to want me to come to his quarters, and I had yet to see the offices and labs of Designer Gene Co. He didn't smile when he greeted me, but then, he never did.

"What's on the menu for today?" he asked mildly, his accent more British than Japanese or Martian. I dialed Bette up on my portable monitor and watched him study her. His face betrayed not the slightest emotion; he didn't even have Rashad's or Mother's professional avidity.

His face was perfect, the template of classical Japanese beauty. It was unaltered, as far as I could tell. The only change that had obviously been made in Hasagawa's appearance may have been made by his parents or grandparents. He was tall.

"What about her nose?" he inquired.

"I had wanted to do *this* with it," I said, showing him the theoretical bump, "but she didn't want that."

"What a shame. She could have been perfect. Perfect." He turned off the monitor and regarded me.

"Would you like some refreshment?" I offered.

"No, thank you," he said without inflection. "I admire your style, Lysel. Your sense of aesthetics is quite harmonious with mine."

"Thank you. When will it be convenient for you to meet with the client?"

He shrugged again. "Anytime."

"Do you prefer day or night?"

"Afternoon, I suppose. You appear to be an afternoon person."

"All right. I'll make the arrangements."

He didn't nod or in any way acknowledge my remark. He simply continued to look me directly in the face as if all responsibility for the conversation rested squarely in my lap; and yet the implication that any *faux pas* on my part would be coolly and thoroughly abhored was implicit in the very set of his graceful head and in the dark pools of his perfect eyes.

I smiled. "When you address Mother, what do you call her? I feel so awkward not knowing her name."

"Perhaps that is what she intends," he said.

"I don't know what you mean."

"Your question has many implications. I've been wondering myself at the true meaning of her refusal to give her name. Is it deep paranoia, the result of living a long life with so many enemies left in one's wake? Or could it be that her return to adolescence is more than skin-deep?"

"Mine is. I feel young again. I feel braver, more energetic—"

"Ah, but this is different, Lysel," he said, with just a trace of energy. "This is *pre*-adolescence. This is that moment when we are poised on the brink, just about to become, just about to transform. Do you remember that time?"

It almost seemed as if he were hanging on my answer. I would have lied, if I could have come up with anything even remotely convincing, but I couldn't.

"No," I said.

"It is extraordinary, like no other time and no other feeling. Most of us don't have time to truly feel the madness of our bodies at that age, but *she*—"

She had all the time in the universe. "Like Hermes," I said.

"What?"

"The Greek messenger god, a beautiful boy who isn't quite a man. As I recall, his hair was even red."

"Yes."

"And what about you, Hasagawa? Do you regret leaving the Hermes time? Or is this where you wanted to be?"

"Are any of us precisely where we want to be?"

"She is."

"Yes," he agreed, without passion. "I think she may be the one creature in this universe who is."

For a moment I felt as if I had really communicated with him. "Thank you," I said. "You've given me something to think about."

But his reply disappointed me. He merely stood and gave me a nod of affirmation, then gracefully turned and left my terrace, as if we hadn't been discussing anything of importance at all, as if he couldn't be troubled to consider what I said or thought.

I couldn't help feeling upset by his behavior. It wasn't that I wanted Hasagawa to treat me as Rashad did, as if he wanted me, or even liked me. But his glacial, lifeless interaction was disturbing. I wondered if his bedside manner would be as unsettling to my clients.

After all, no one likes to be treated as if they're already dead.

*   *   *

I made an appointment with Bette for a meeting the very next day, but it was preempted by the dust storm.

I was first aware of it when I woke to darkness. I had been aware of a howling for some time, had even incorporated it into my dream as the sound of those vacuuming men I always saw on the street. I dreamed they were out on my terrace, cleaning, and I wanted to get up and tell them to stop. I was so determined to do so that I finally woke up.

I got up and looked out my windows. I saw an astonishing swirl of shifting matter, and for several moments I just stood, uncomprehendingly. Then my vidphone sounded. Mother was on the line.

"Sometime today you ought to come up and look at the weather screen," she said.

"Will it still be blowing in a couple of hours?" I asked.

She laughed. "Our dust storms have been known to last for months."

I was speechless for several moments, but her sharp eyes prodded me back to life. "How do you keep this city running under those conditions?" I asked.

"You'll see," she said, and signed off.

Reddish-purple color throbbed on my walls.

I wandered into the bathroom and flipped on the light, relieved to have the brightness on my face. In the month that had passed since my awakening, my skin had regained its normal color, and I had a healthy, rosy underglow.

When I had been a video prostitute, I had kept a rigid morning routine which always started with careful inspection of my face and body for signs of aging or dimpling. I still followed those habits. I stretched, bent over in different angles, sat, lay down, kneeled on hands and knees. My body looked perfect from every angle, my face was fresh and unlined, unswollen by sleep.

My breasts still felt almost weightless. The combination of implant suspension and Martian gravity gave them an unreal beauty; yet when I touched them, they were as yielding as they were supposed to be. My skin was petal soft, my nipples were sensitive and reacted instantly to stimulation. I looked at them and touched them, noticing at the same time how slender my hands were, admiring the soft fall of my hair about my shoulders and down my back, a waterfall that gave me a femininity I would have scorned back in my butch-cut days. But now I liked it.

I slowly knelt on the rug with my knees apart, until I was sitting on my heels. Something new was happening. I was aroused at the sight of myself. I had never felt that way before, never been anything but clinical about my image; but now it almost seemed that the person in the mirror was separate from me, a lovely stranger whose most intimate secrets I wanted to see exposed.

I rubbed and caressed my breasts, sometimes softly and sometimes roughly, flicking my nails across my nipples until they were swollen and rosy. They bounced slightly, trembled with my movements, and the sight of my hands on them had me gasping with pleasure. I ran a hand down my body and between my legs, over my vulva, spreading it open until it looked like a shell, a hot little flower full of dew. I took the wetness up to my clitoris, and moaned with surprise and delight. My nails were painted a pearly pink. I watched them disappear into my vagina and reappear again, glistening.

I couldn't get enough of myself. The last time I had been this excited was in the helicraft with Rico; and before that it was the time in the chairs, with Joe. The face I imagined watching me now belonged to both of them, sometimes shy, sometimes feral and approving.

They grinned as I stroked myself toward climax. They licked their lips as I moved my hips in slow, controlled movements, like a naked belly dancer on her knees, until my entire body was trembling with the effort of delaying my orgasm. But it couldn't be delayed forever, and when it came, I watched every flicker and tremble in my face, in my body. And I saw what my vagina looked like in orgasm. That was fascinating.

Afterward, I sat back, still enthralled with the sight of myself, and thought about all of those years I had performed for my video customers. Now I knew what they had seen when they watched me, what they had felt. The idea was so exciting, I almost started all over again; but I couldn't go on like that all day long. I almost felt that if I let myself, I wouldn't be able to stop masturbating, stop looking at myself. It was as if my adolescence was asserting itself the way it had never been able to the first time around. Something had thwarted it, and now it wanted its due. And I, who had always loved to look at things, was a captive audience.

I made myself get up and get into the shower. I didn't make it a cold shower—that seemed unnecessary, not to mention unhelpful. The cold water would have made my nipples stand up, and the sight of those rosy creatures was irresistible. I stared straight ahead and washed in as businesslike a fashion as I could; but I still had little aftershocks when I touched my vulva, even though I was only there for the sake of cleanliness. I let myself enjoy it anyway.

It wasn't until I was getting dressed that it occurred to me to wonder if Mother or Rashad had watched my performance from a monitor. Or Hasagawa. The idea of the men looking was pleasant, but the same imagined scenario with Mother drew no reaction from me at all. I should have thought I would feel ashamed, disturbed at the suggestion of such symbolic incest, but I felt absolutely nothing. Empty.

In my mind, the image of Joe/Rico was still watching me, as if waiting for my question. *Am I sick?* I asked them. *Am I so different from other people?*

I don't care, I heard Rico saying, just like when he had kissed me in the helicraft. But he faded away before his lips touched mine, leaving me with yet another new sensation.

Loneliness. But that was one I didn't want. I ran out the door, hoping to leave it behind with the mirror.

The weather screen, and the room in which it was located, was not so easy to find. I knocked on Mother's door and on the doors of every suite on the way back to my quarters, but no one answered. As soon as I got back to my own suite I realized I didn't have vidphone codes to any of the other levels in that building. I called Mother's suite, despite the fact that

I was pretty sure she wasn't in there. Of course she didn't answer.

The storm howled outside my windows.

I hadn't bothered to turn the lights on in the rest of my suite, but the bathroom light shone in a jagged path from my bedroom and out into the living room. I sat down on the bed and looked at it for a while. For some reason, it was soothing, like a meditation mantra. I just looked and looked, and my mind was calm.

I had always been fascinated by images. Having my art collection back had brought me far more happiness than I had ever thought I could feel. The tall windows in the hallway delighted me, and a simple thing like the angle of light and dark on my floor was now giving me great satisfaction. I don't know how long I sat there—I didn't get up again until my foot had fallen asleep.

I limped into my living room, and regarded the storm from those windows. It hadn't varied in intensity at all, at least not as far as my eyes and ears could detect. What must it look like on the satellite screen? It would be beautiful, like those metamorphosing-impressionist light paintings people had been so fond of in the mid-twenty-first century. I really wanted to see it.

So I left my suite again, and this time I approached the forbidden zone.

It wasn't that Mother had warned me away from anything. She hadn't said, "Don't come into the labs, don't go through this door or that one." It's just that I was fairly sure she was going to kill me sooner or later, and I didn't want to rush things.

But I wasn't terribly concerned about death as I

walked down those halls toward the door I'd never opened. I was a little excited, in fact. Thinking back, I was very much like a rat in a maze, about to find the cheese. I passed Mother's suite, and Rashad's, which was at the very end of the hall, and there was the door. I put my hand on the knob, turned it . . .

And it was locked. There wasn't a lock panel on it, so I hadn't expected that. There wasn't an old fashioned keyhole lock on it either, so how did it function?

A beam of light suddenly hit me in the middle of my chest. It flickered for about twenty seconds, and then died again. From somewhere inside the door, a dissonant chime complained.

It was a retinal lock, and I wasn't even in the right position for it to scan me and turn me down. Finally I had found an honest-to-God security system. I shrugged and started to walk away, then stopped when I heard a sound. I thought it was coming from behind the door, that perhaps someone was coming to see who had annoyed the lock. I put on my best face and waited.

But the sound wasn't coming from behind the door. It was coming from all the way down the hall, around the corner, past my suite. And it was going CLUNK, CLUNK, CLUNK, CLUNK . . .

Scorpianne?

I dashed for Rashad's door. It was locked. Mother's was locked, too, and the door farther down the hall, near the corner. The footsteps were almost there now—so I dashed back to the retinal lock and turned the knob again, practically spraining my wrist in the process. That tripped the light, and I moved my eye into the beam. CLUNK, CLUNK, CLUNK, CLUNK. The footsteps neared the corner.

The door made the sound of rejection. I hoped it would trip another alarm and someone would come see what was going on, if they didn't already know. Behind me, the footsteps rounded the corner, CLUNK, CLUNK, CLUNK—then suddenly stopped.

Scorpianne was looking at me now. Whatever she was, flesh or robot, Mother or someone else, I was finally going to meet her. I looked over my shoulder.

But she wasn't there. The devil had come in her place.

That was the first thought that popped into my head. He was a red giant, with horns on his head, growing on either side of a black widow's peak. His features were long and sensual, but had an oddly innocent beauty. He seemed stunned at the sight of me as he stared with burning, yellow eyes. They were so arresting, I almost didn't notice that he was naked.

When he began to walk again, I saw his hooves. They made the CLUNK, CLUNK as he moved cautiously toward me, as if he were afraid I might try to get away from him. As he moved closer, his penis got harder, until it was finally so hard that it barely bounced at all as he moved. It was enormous, transfixing.

What incredible work it must have been to change him from a man into—*this*. How could they have done it? How could they have caused him to grow those hooves where his feet used to be? It was staggering.

When I was able to look at his face again, I saw his smile, and knew that at least it wasn't murder he had on his mind. He was a sex god. They must have changed his mind, too. They must have changed his *brian*.

"Come here," he said, his voice low and huge and perfectly masculine. He reached for me, and an intoxicating odor enveloped me, a cloud of sexual perfume.

Someone seized me from behind and pulled me backward, through the open doorway. I flailed my arms and landed right on my augmented butt.

"Wait!" cried the red giant, just as Mother slammed the door in his face.

She smiled down at me. "He's dangerous, dear. You shouldn't play with him. Besides, he's mine."

Faintly, through the door, I could hear him crying.

I wasn't sure what to ask Mother as we walked up that hall together, or if I should ask anything at all. She hadn't said anything more than "Come on, let's go see the screen" before she was off again, maintaining her usual slightly superior position as we walked.

Finally I asked, "So what am I supposed to do if I see him in the hall again?"

"You won't," she said. "Someone forgot to lock the garden door. They won't forget again."

I was sure they wouldn't.

"He was crying," I said.

"He's very emotional."

We went through another series of doors, then into a luxurious and spectacular viewing room. The screen most people would use to watch movies was a satellite monitor here. Below it were about two dozen technicians at consoles, all looking at small screens of their own, all speaking on headsets, and all very busy. The rest of the room was taken up by couches, cushions, and refreshment-laden tables. A number of beautiful people were sprawled about, including the black and green couple Mother had pointed out in the cafe a month before. They both stared at me intently.

"Let me introduce you to the Finklesteins," said Mother. "They're very anxious to meet you."

I had a premonition about who the Finklesteins would turn out to be; sure enough, as we strolled over to their couch, the black and green couple rose to meet us.

"Gawd," said the green girl, in an accent that anyone would recognize as New York, her lovely Chinese face frowning with dismay as she looked me up and down. "I sure hope you're not a *body* sculptor."

"Face sculpting is my specialty," I said, extending a hand for her to shake. She took it absently while she gave my face a second look.

"Don't mind my wife," said Mr. Finklestein, with the same accent. "She isn't known for her tact." He extended his hand too, and I shook it as well.

"If you don't mind my asking— " I began.

"Yes, we're Jewish," said the green girl. "We've been totally overhauled."

"Meyer and Lisa were the first customers to buy Rashad's virus," said Mother. "They've had many other things done, too."

Meyer and Lisa gave Mother nervous glances before turning back to me.

"Why would you give yourself tits like that?" Lisa asked me.

"I was a video prostitute for many years. They improved my business."

I had thought that might shock her into silence, but instead she said, "You used one of those Machines in your business? Meyer and I used to have a few. We used them all the time, but we got bored with them."

I wasn't sure I wanted to know where one went from there. "May I ask— " I began.

"I'm fifty-eight," said Lisa. "Meyer's sixty-two."

"I would never have guessed."

"Well, I hope not. We paid a goddam fortune for this look."

"I have some others I want Lysel to meet," said Mother, and Lisa took a step backward. Meyer was gripping her gently by the upper arm now, and he smiled at Mother with perfect teeth. "Nice to meet you, Lysel," he said, though he wasn't looking at me.

"Nice to meet you, too," I said, as Mother guided me away from them.

"Do you know what he wanted done first?" she whispered to me as we crossed the room.

I guessed. "A bigger penis?"

"That's what men *always* ask for first!" she giggled. "Even if they've already got big ones."

"What do they ask for second?"

She shrugged. "It depends."

"How about hooves?"

She cocked her head and smiled. "Now you're getting the idea."

But somehow I had a feeling I wasn't getting it at all.

The weather screen was all that I had hoped for and more, but it wasn't long before my attention was snagged by the smaller screens and the technicians below it. Only a few of them appeared to be looking at the storm from various viewpoints. Others were displaying quite different views of Mars, including one that was apparently positioned over the North Pole.

Mother was flirting with a young man who, judging from his conversation, might actually be a real adolescent. I turned my eye to the other loungers and saw a man watching the screens intently. He was wearing a conservative suit, not fashionable and not tailored. He wasn't drinking anything, and there was a lively intelligence in his eyes. I wandered over to him and sat down.

"Say," I said, after a few moments, "are those all satellite pictures?"

He wrenched his attention away from the screen and studied me as if I were an unexpected specimen who had wandered under his microscope. He was handsome, but in an absentminded, washed-out sort of way, and he apparently felt it was all right to look as if he were about thirty.

"And you are— ?" he drawled.

"Lucy Cartier," I said. "I'm a face sculptor."

"Well, you look like one," he said, and returned to his scrutiny of the screens. I thought I would have to move on, but suddenly he added, "No, they're not all satellite hookups, my dear. Some of them are direct from the orbital colony. That's one of the few worthwhile things those arrogant bums do to justify their existence out there."

"Oh," I said, and leaned toward the screens as if I were fascinated. Actually I was, but I wanted to know some things too. "Do all Martians have this kind of access to satellite information?"

He snorted. "No, my dear, they do not." He looked sideways at me again. "I gather you are *not* a Martian."

"I'm an Earthling," I said, careful not to put too much cutesy into the statement.

"Ah," he nodded. "At least you're not a Jovian."

"No," I smiled. "In fact, I went into regeneration just as that micro-war on Ganymede broke out. I don't even know how it ended."

"Is that so," he said, in a tone that warned me he knew perfectly well I was fishing for information.

"Yes. I'd like your opinion on the subject."

"Really? And you don't even know me. Well, that's all right; I'm sure if you did, you wouldn't want my opinion after all. This gives me a chance to shoot my mouth off."

"Please do."

He turned slightly toward me, but not so much so that he couldn't look at the screens from time to time too. "I'm Red Hulot—that's with a *t* on the end, not a *w*—I'm into transport and energy conversion."

He shook my hand as if I were a fellow business associate, and I made sure my grip was firm. "Asteroids?" I guessed.

"Among other things, yes, but I'm not one of those idiots who fought with the miners on Ganymede. Let me tell you something. If they had just made a few more concessions to begin with, that war never would have broken out."

"The miners?"

"No, the Jovian business consortium."

"I didn't know there was a Jovian business consortium."

"Frankly, that's the polite name. I've got a few others for those bloodsucking bastards. I lost some good men in that damned war—Jeff Barnum was one of my top lawyers, poor son of a gun was one of the first hostages they killed after the initial proposal was turned down. Those damned idiots think you can sacrifice good people for nothing!"

"But if you're an asteroid transporter, weren't you part of the consortium?"

"Hell, yes, I'm part of *three* consortiums, including the Mars, but I don't have a majority vote." Crow's-feet crinkled at the corners of his eyes as he gave me a grin that looked half-pleased, half-frustrated.

"What kind of concessions should they have made?"

"Youth Technology, for one. Give those poor bastards some reason to believe they have a nicer future, somewhere else, once they retire. No one wants to work themselves to death and have nothing to show for it!"

"That sounds logical. What else?"

He counted the points on his fingers. "One: low-interest loans for their kids' education. Two: a ten percent pay raise. Three: an improved health care plan including at least some rudimentary Youth treatments. Four: a price ceiling from Jovian merchants who supply basic needs. Five: retirement at fifty-five with free transport off Ganymede if they want it. Six: a forty percent pension for five years, so they can get settled in other jobs." He gave me another one of those half-and-half grins.

"Our local miners already have that kind of deal

with us. We could have swallowed those costs easily—hell!—the cost of the war in the first week alone would have paid for the next two decades! Damned idiots thought they could make themselves some slaves out of those miners and do what they wanted. Well, you can push people just so far, and then—boom!"

He glanced back at the screens, as if looking for the results of the explosion. I looked too, but couldn't find what he saw there.

"Did the miners get any of those concessions?"

"The ringleaders were executed. That was stupid; now they've got themselves some martyrs. They got their pay raise, but they've got heavy fines to pay. It's just a matter of time before they make another bid for power. Shit, those people wrangle asteroids! All they have to do is slingshot a few of those Atens in our direction; we'd have all we could do just to change their trajectory—"

"Atens?"

"Those asteroids cross into the orbits of the inner planets all the time. Still a lot of 'em left, too, and they travel *fast*. Remember what happened to the dinosaurs?"

"Believe it or not, I wasn't there."

He laughed. "Hell, I know you can't be as old as me. I'm seventy-two."

So maybe he wasn't entirely disdainful of Mother's viruses.

"Regeneration?" I asked lightly.

"Hell, yes. Good when you need a long rest. How old are you, Lucy?"

"Fifty-six."

"Good. I hate flirting with kids. Not that my wife

wouldn't kill me if she caught me doing it. You come to Mars just to get into the sculpting biz?"

"Mother brought me here."

"Mother?"

I nodded in her direction. He followed my look, and his face became very serious. "Shit," he said.

"I like to warn people."

"That's mighty kind of you. Jesus, I can't imagine that little body giving birth to a baby. It boggles the mind."

"I'm not so sure she ever did."

He gave me a raised-eyebrow kind of look. "It's like that, huh?"

"Yes."

"Well, Lucy, you have my sympathy. I'll tell you honestly, if that little lady didn't have the best Youth Technology to offer, I wouldn't have a damned thing to do with her. Hell, I don't even know her name!"

"Does anybody?"

"One or two military muckety-mucks. Maybe. That's my guess. These are their satellites, you know."

"No, I didn't know."

"After the war, the Mars business consortium was the only funding those guys were getting. Even the interim government couldn't get money from Earth, but that's for the best. We own ourselves, and now we own them too."

It was my turn to raise my eyebrows.

"Hey, little lady, didn't I just get through telling you what patience and a few concessions can do for you?"

"Yes. Thank you."

"I'll take that as sincere," he said, and he was right.

"What with all they have to put up with," I mused, "it's a wonder that Jovian miners don't go freelance, undercut everyone else's prices ..."

"Now, honey," drawled Mr. Hulot, "*that's* something that would be worth going to war over."

He said it as charmingly as he had said everything else, but I didn't take it as a joke. The screen across the room erupted in a sudden burst of new chaos, as if reading our minds.

The storm raged on through the next several days, and I found out about the *other* Mars. The underground one.

The subway wasn't the only option for transportation, even during the worst weather. I took a storm car to my office on the second day to get some files. The car was like a giant bullet with a diamond-glass top. Its magnetic wheels kept it firmly on the pig-iron roads, and its directional system kept me from hitting other storm cars as it took me to my underground lot.

But I quickly found out that most of my clients didn't want to meet me there when the wind was blowing. Not when we could use the trendy liaison offices in the underground facilities.

"I've never been down here!" gushed Bette Rodriguez when I finally met with her on the third day of the storm. "Not past the subway, anyway. I hear the restaurants are so expensive, they don't even list the prices on the menus."

"There are some affordable restaurants down here," I assured her. "In the G and H sections, at least. I passed them on the way here."

"But I bet the food isn't as good."

"The food is every bit as good. Some of it is better."

She looked at me nervously, and I made a mental note not to say things like that to my richer clients. It's just that I didn't want Bette to think she had to go hungry just because she was only earning a few hundred thousand a year.

"You'll like Dr. Hasagawa," I started to say, when Bette suddenly sat up straighter in her chair. I looked over my shoulder, and there was the doctor, coming in from the outer office. He ran his cool glance over both of us as he entered the room and slid gracefully into a chair.

"Doctor Hasagawa," I said, "this is Bette Rodriguez."

He ignored Bette and said, "This office is rather shabby, don't you think?"

"No, I don't. It's a bit sterile, but 'shabby' is not the word for it at all. Can we get down to business?"

The iron in my voice seemed to have an effect. He looked at Bette and gave her a slight bow, from his chair. "I apologize if I seemed to imply anything rude with my comment, Ms. Rodriguez," he said, his tone as icy as ever.

"That's okay," she stammered.

"Dr. Hasagawa is going to need to get a close look at your face and ask you some medical questions," I told Bette.

"I brought a hard copy of my medical file." She plopped it down on the desk. "In case I can't remember something."

"I'll study it back at my office." Hasagawa got up and moved to the chair next to Bette. He immediately put his hands on her face and began to explore it. She cringed.

"I'm sorry if this troubles you," he said. "I need to know what I'm going to be working with."

"That's okay," she stammered again.

My own doctor had done this with me back on Earth, so I knew Hasagawa wasn't copping a feel. Not that his touch could be construed as anything but impersonal to begin with.

"Have you ever been on anti-depressants?"

"No," she said.

"Medication for diabetes?"

"No."

"Schizophrenia?"

"No."

And he named dozens of other medications and conditions while she said no, no, no, and he continued to probe her face. Finally he pinched a little of it between thumb and forefinger and said, "Olive skin like yours has a tendency to form keloid scars."

"I've been told that wouldn't be a problem," she said anxiously.

"No, it's not a problem. But you need to be made aware of the medication we use during the sculpting to prevent the scarring. It's the law."

"Okay."

And that's how the rest of the examination went. Bette turned from a confident, beautiful professional woman into a meek little girl under Hasagawa's touch. I could understand it. After all, he was the one who held her looks in his hands—literally, at the moment. She was relieved when it was all over and she could go.

"How does a week from today sound?" he asked her. "Three o'clock?"

"Perfect," she said, as she dashed out the door.

He let his eyes settle back on me, and for a moment I saw something behind them. He had enjoyed himself. Not the touching, but the discomfort he had caused.

"Would you like to have lunch with me?" I asked him.

"I don't eat lunch."

"Do you eat breakfast? Or dinner?"

He gave me a smile that managed to look tolerant. "No. Food is vulgar, don't you think? Eating it, smelling it, chewing it. Digesting it."

"I like it. I find it a great pleasure. You must have an obsessive-compulsive disorder or you would too."

"Do you seriously believe that I would allow myself to be manipulated by a disease that could easily be cured with simple anti-depressants?"

"You would if it fit in with your sense of aesthetics."

He studied me. Another man might have leaned back, lit a cigarette, done things to mask his nervousness while pretending to be cool. But Hasagawa had no nervousness to hide. He merely looked and measured.

"You think I'm your enemy, Lysel. But I'm actually the closest thing you've got to a friend at Designer Gene Co.," he said at last.

"How close is close?"

"Not very," he admitted. "But I'm not going to go out of my way to harm you."

"Who is?"

"Whom do you think?"

"I want to hear you say it."

He shrugged.

"What's her real name?" I demanded.

"Don't expect to get information out of me. You know only slightly less than I do about the situation."

If that was true, he was actually telling me a lot. He picked up Bette's file and stood.

"You're not the burned-out whore we all thought you would be," he said.

When I didn't react, he turned smoothly and walked out the door.

I was eating lunch in one of the medium-priced underground cafes when I saw a face that looked familiar.

He was tall and thin, with short blond hair and colorless features, dressed like a businessman. He was looking at me as if he knew me but didn't intend to say hello. I looked back, trying to place him from one of the other cafes, or the shops, or even one of Mother's parties. He belonged somewhere in the past, but where?

I didn't want him to think my stare was an invitation, so I looked down and concentrated on the second half of my chicken walnut salad on orbital croissant. I had almost finished the last bite when I placed him.

The last time I had seen him was on my vidphone back on Earth. He had been saying, "We don't respond graciously to threats."

I looked up again to make sure it was the same executive, but he was gone by then. I looked everywhere for him, even studied the crowds that were filing by, but I didn't see him. Somehow, though, I had a feeling he could see me.

I left the cafe and joined the crowd that was heading for the train terminals. I had intended to do a little shopping first, but that feeling of being watched had me jangled. I put on my most aggressive stride and plowed through the crowd, grateful for the mysterious disappearance of my touching phobia as I rubbed shoulders and thighs with passersby. I was almost to my terminal when I saw someone else I recognized. He was about a hundred feet ahead of me, walking fast.

"Joe!" I called, and started to run.

He plowed ahead, increasing his pace. He was headed for a pedestrian crossing point; any moment the light would turn red, and he would be through ahead of me. I would lose him while waiting for the green light, I was sure of it.

"Joe!" I broke into a flat-out run. He was running himself now, his long muscular legs eating up ground as he dashed for the crossing point. He would just make the light.

"Joe!" I screamed, one more time, then suddenly heard what name I was calling. I wanted to knock my head back into proper working order as I cried, "Rico, wait!"

Rico turned around and saw me. His eyes widened with shock, then his face stiffened. He didn't look happy to see me, but he waited until I had caught up with him. I stopped about three feet from him, breathing heavily, and studied his angry face. There wasn't a trace of welcome in his eyes.

"Captain—" I began.

"Don't call me that," he snapped, and pointed to

his bars of rank on his sleeve. I noticed one bar had been stripped away recently. "I'm a lieutenant now," he said.

I didn't really need to ask, but I did anyway, "Why?"

"Conduct unbecoming to an officer," he said.

"She could have done worse, you know." I glanced at the people swarming around us, wishing they weren't there.

"No," he said. "I didn't know. But I'm learning."

"Could we find a place to talk alone?"

He looked like he was going to tell me to go to hell. But instead he said, "Sure. This way."

I followed him. We walked back up the hallway and onto the office concourse again. He didn't speak to me or look at me the whole time. We went into some offices that Hasagawa would have been right about if he had called them shabby.

"These are vacant right now," he said, directing me to a chair next to a scarred table. The table looked like it had had computer equipment sitting on it recently. He sat in the chair opposite me. "Now what's on your mind?" he demanded.

"These were military offices?" I asked.

"Yes."

"Could they be bugged?"

"Why would they be bugged?"

"Why would you be demoted just for kissing me?"

He frowned, then shrugged. "I picked this office at random. Even I didn't know I was going to use it."

That would have to do. I leaned on the table with my chin in my hands and thought about what to say to him. Before I could think of anything, he asked, "Why haven't you called me?"

"I was trying to set up my office—"

"Bullshit. It's been over a month. I got demoted for you, and I didn't even get the time of day out of you."

His hostility was making me want to cry, but I held the tears back and let him tell me off.

"I earned my rank," he said, his voice beginning to crack. "I shot down ten enemy craft in the Jovian conflict—"

"Wait!" I had to interrupt him. "The Jovian conflict?"

"Yes!"

"When was that?"

"Where the hell have you been? Oh, yeah, I forgot. Rejuvenation, getting your phony skin to look young so people won't know what an old broad you are. I know your age, Lucy. I looked it up."

There were unshed tears in his eyes, but I had to know what he was talking about.

"Where did you shoot down the enemy craft?" I demanded.

"Just outside Mars orbit."

"They were from Ganymede?"

"From Earth."

That made me sit back and think. Joe had said Mars might back the Ganymede miners against Earth. But Red Hulot had led me to believe that the Ganymede micro-war had fizzled out. "So there was a war after all."

Rico snorted with disgust. "A war. We engaged Earth fighters twice, and we beat the crap out of them. They went home and said, 'Can we talk about this?'"

"You sound disappointed."

He glared at me bitterly.

"You say you looked up my age," I prompted.

"Fifty-six," he snapped.

"How did you get the information?"

"I used the call-girl picture file for Earth," he said. "Video division."

"That's the only division there is."

"Not anymore."

"Really? Things have changed even more than I thought. What else did you learn about me?"

"Lucy Cartier," he recited. "You arrived in Phoenix, Arizona, from Mars at the age of sixteen. You had recently been cured of the Blue Clap. You filed for a video prostitute's license and set up shop immediately. You kept the same residence and the same job for thirty-eight years before you retired."

"The file said I retired?"

"Yes."

"Then why was there a file to begin with?"

He looked grimly triumphant. "I've got a buddy in communications. We found out they keep those files for old clients who might want to get in touch with retired prostitutes."

I must have looked horrified, because he relented. "You didn't know about that," he said.

"No. But I'd like to talk to that buddy of yours."

He didn't answer. I could tell he regretted telling me anything at all. But it was too late, he could see that. The realization was dawning on his handsome, bitter face.

"I wish I'd never laid eyes on you," he said.

"I wish you hadn't either. But since you did, here's the story. I *was* a video prostitute. I left the business when one of my clients tried to kill me with my

Machine. The Machine had been rigged by special arrangement with Machine Co., for rich clients who wanted a snuff experience. You following me so far?"

"Machine Co.?" he said, looking puzzled.

"Yes. They're the ones who make all of the Machines currently in use on Earth— "

"Designer Gene Co. owns Machine Co.," he said. "Why would your own mother try to kill you?"

My head was going numb, from my temples all the way down to the nape of my neck. Another piece of the puzzle had just landed squarely on my head, but I didn't know what to do with it.

He put his hand on mine, but the gesture wasn't meant to be comforting. "I can check on your story, you know," he warned.

"No, you can't."

"My buddy— "

"What do you think the record's going to say? 'Ms. Cartier retired when an attempt was made on her life by Machine Co.'? You could find that if you went deep enough; but if you do, they'll be looking for *you*. You have a lot more to lose than your rank, Joe. You and your buddy, both."

"Are you threatening me?"

"No!" I shrieked. "No! You big, stupid dope, I'm trying to warn you!"

"Why would you care?"

This time I couldn't stop my crying. So I ignored it. "I don't want any more of my friends to die," I said. "Not because of some damned business venture."

My tears seemed to scare him away. He looked at me soberly for several minutes while I thought about what I should do next. He was still holding my hand.

"What are you going to do?" he asked me.

"I don't know."

"When we leave here, I won't see you again."

"No one may ever see me again."

That wasn't what he wanted to hear. He kept hold of my hand as he walked around the table and stood over me. "Right here," he said.

"What?"

"I want you. Right here. If I'm going to be demoted for conduct unbecoming to an officer, I might as well engage in a little conduct."

I didn't know what to say, but my body did. My nipples instantly got hard. He looked down at them, as if they had winked at him. "In the back," he said. "The rooms have locks back there."

I let him draw me out of the chair and down a dark hall. We went into a back room, and he switched on a light. "I want to see you," he said, as he locked the door. Then he began to undress.

I watched him. His resemblance to Joe was more pronounced when he was being aggressive. He *moved* like Joe, and as he pulled off his pants, I almost laughed at the sight of a familiar friend.

"Take off your clothes," said Rico.

I did, giving him a nice show. He enjoyed it, but he didn't touch me yet. I wondered why, until I suddenly understood. "I want you too," I said.

"Say my name."

"I want you, Rico."

He still didn't move, and I was at a loss. He was supposed to take me in his arms now, kiss me, fondle my breasts. That's the way it happened in erotic fiction, at least in the kind written before the Machine revolution. He looked so handsome standing there.

He smelled so good. I wanted to feel his skin, so I did. I reached out and put my hand on his chest. He leaned into my touch, slightly, and his breathing became harsher.

I took a step toward him, then another, until we were only a few inches apart. His hands stayed at his sides, but they twitched. *What do you want to do?* I asked myself. His face was what interested me the most. So I put my hands on it. I felt the roughness where his whiskers were growing just beneath his skin. I felt his firm jawline, brushed my fingers over his mouth. His tongue touched my fingertips, and a warm shock went through my nerves.

I moved until my body was pressed against his. He was hot, his muscles hard. They trembled against my skin, but still he didn't touch me with his hands. His eyes seemed to swallow me whole, yet at the same time they invited me into him, a red, pulsing place.

I rubbed his short hair, so thick and black and shiny, feeling the shape of his beautiful head. I let my hand wander down the back of his neck and pulled his face down to mine. I kissed his mouth, plundering it the same way Joe had plundered mine all of those times, and I finally understood why he had liked it when I had simply stood there, yielding, as Rico was yielding now.

"You're so beautiful," I panted. "You're such a man. So big and strong."

I felt a dampness against my belly where his penis was pressed. I eased the pressure there slightly. I wanted this to last as long as it could. I kissed his neck, breathing in the male scent, losing myself in the pleasure.

"Lucy," he breathed into my ear. "Baby."

His hands finally moved, tangling themselves in my hair and pulling my head back so he could kiss my mouth. His kisses were still different from Joe's; they were his own, emotional and somehow shy, as if he were angry with me yet also afraid to hurt me. But he still didn't touch the rest of my body, and I sensed he wanted me to keep taking the initiative.

So I drew him to the floor, and gently pushed him onto his back. I began to kiss him, starting with his nipples and working my way down. His hands finally found my breasts, and I watched him to see how he looked at them. I could see he liked them best of all, so I dangled them over his mouth, letting him get a good, long taste, before I pulled away and began my descent a second time. His hands stroked my wet nipples, adding a new definition of delight to my experience.

His body tasted like salt and sex, like man. I kissed his penis gently, then teased it with soft little licks, as delicately as I could, just enough to keep it hard.

"Let me inside you," he moaned.

I poised over him. This was it, this was my first time. I hadn't thought of it quite that way before—how could I after thirty-eight years as a prostitute? But this was my first *real* penis. The first I could remember, anyway. I wanted to savor it all the way in.

"Tell me how much you want it," he demanded.

"I want it more than anything." I pushed my vagina against the head of his penis, just swallowing the head. "Fuck me, Rico."

His penis slid inside me, stroking my insides with

a hot friction that was utterly unlike the cold, quick slide of metal.

"I'm better than him," he moaned. "Tell me I'm better than that other guy."

"You don't have to be anyone else, Rico," I said, feeling myself losing control, feeling the climax rushing over me.

"Tell me!" he pleaded.

But I couldn't tell him what I didn't know. I just couldn't.

"How was he, dear?" asked Mother, at supper.

I finished chewing and took a sip of wine before I answered her.

"None of your business," I said.

She smiled, and toyed with the single lock of red hair that dangled from her elaborate coif. "But I'm your mother."

I dabbed at my mouth with the napkin, then sat up and looked her right in the eye.

"Let's set some ground rules around here," I said.

"Oh, *let's*," she mocked.

"I'm fifty-six years old, and I don't have to explain anything about my life to you."

"Is that so?" She cocked her head.

"Yes. If you can't respect my privacy, I'm going to leave. It's as simple as that."

"And why haven't you left before now?"

I kept my gaze steady. "You went to a lot of trouble to bring me here. I wanted to respect your feelings. But I'd like you to respect mine as well."

Mother's smile was lazy as she toyed with some red citrus. "You still seem like a child to me," she sighed. "Especially when you look the way you do now."

"You'll have to get over that feeling."

"I can't. No, Lysel, I'm afraid I simply can't." She batted her lashes at me. "What are you going to do about it?"

"I suppose I'll have to move into my own apartment."

"Just try it," she teased. "I dare you."

I didn't answer, and she seemed to get bored with the game. "Oh, do what you like," she pouted. "I don't care. I just wanted to know if you enjoyed him. After all, he's *gorgeous*. If I could grow men like him, we wouldn't need to manufacture Machines anymore."

"From what I hear, Machines are going out of style, anyway."

"Really, Lysel," Mother purred. "If you want me to treat you like an adult in this business, you should learn some things about it. Take the concept of market saturation, for instance."

Something told me another puzzle piece was about to fall on my head.

"I'm willing to learn," I said.

She spooned some sugar into her tea and stirred it daintily. "The term practically explains itself. Once the market is saturated with a product, demand begins to decline. The funny thing about the sex industry, my dear, is what's considered taboo today becomes tomorrow's mad passion. Machines were considered very perverse in the beginning, you know."

"I never thought of them that way."

"No, of course not! You had just recovered from the Blue Clap. That little disease set off quite a chain reaction in the Machine business." She giggled reminiscently.

I drank my sweetened tea, but it was sour in my mouth.

"It helped," she continued, "that so many people seemed to develop a phobia about physical contact. That was a convenient side-effect."

"I see what you mean. But all that's past now. What's next on the horizon, Mother?"

She grinned at me impishly. "Lysel, you silly goose, you've already met him!"

Like an idiot, I assumed she was talking about Rico. When I didn't answer, she jumped to her feet and said, "Finish your supper here if you like, dear. I've got some unfinished business in the labs."

"All right."

"You may want to go up to the weather room afterward. I hear Olympus Mons is erupting again. That's always good for a cheap thrill or two." She danced to the door and paused there, looking at me over one small shoulder. "And think about what I've said, will you, Lysel? I want so much for you to follow in my footsteps."

"I want that too, Mother."

She blew me a kiss, and scampered out the door.

I waited about thirty seconds, and then I followed her.

Despite my best efforts, I lost Mother almost immediately. She went through the retinal-lock door, and by the time I got it to open for me, the hall was empty. I went on up to the weather room anyway; after all, I'd been specifically invited. Hasagawa was there with three women, and all four of them were completely engrossed in the screen. The technicians, as always, were too busy to notice anyone coming in or out of the room. I wondered if they ever left it themselves.

The three women might have been doctors. They had Hasagawa's aloof demeanor, as well as Ann's air of professionalism. None of them looked to be over twenty, of course.

I pretended to watch the eruption on the screen for a while—not difficult to do, since it was utterly spectacular. But pretty soon I realized that none of them gave a damn about what I was doing anyway, so I went back out into the hall.

I tried several doors along the way back, mostly out of boredom, since I didn't really believe that any of them would open for me. But I was wrong. One *did* open. I went through it, into darkness, and heard the distant sound of panting.

I closed the door behind me and listened for a moment. Someone was getting a good workout. Two someones, in fact, a man and a woman. I tiptoed down the darkened hall, past more closed doors, and around a corner. Up ahead, a bar of light revealed a door that hadn't been properly closed. I crept up to it and peered through the crack.

The red man was naked and tied to a table by his ankles and his wrists. On top of him, equally naked, was Mother. His penis was thrusting as far inside her as it could go, apparently only about two-thirds of the way, and she was riding him like he was a stallion, clinging to her perch for dear life while he fucked her so wildly it seemed his restraints were ready to burst. Both of them were moaning, gasping, and having a very good time.

But she teased him. She leaned over him as if she were going to let him lick her delicate nipples. He strained his head up as far as it would go and tried desperately to taste her, but she kept them just out of reach. He could barely touch them with the tip of his tongue, no more. She would pull her vagina off of him completely and hold it just out of reach as well; then suddenly envelop him and fuck him as hard as she could. He wept with frustration and adoration.

I supposed I ought to have felt appalled at the sight of my mother having sex with a red demon, but I had no real concept of *Mother* to begin with, no memories of nurturing, punishment, reassurance. I only knew the Mother in the works of the masters down through the ages, the Da Vincis and Botticellis. I tried to compare this scene with one of those, to no avail. Perhaps this was the new Mother, the ageless Mother, no longer a virgin or even a grown woman. The Mother who cares more about her Venus Mons than any Olympus Mons.

The red demon threw his head back, and his long black hair streamed over the edge of the table. He thrust his magnificent pelvis at Mother, impaling her little vagina and pushing her up into the air. She clawed at his skin and laughed, then cried, "Oh, oh!"

"Mother!" he moaned, and came like a runaway train.

Mother.

Meaning that the red man strapped to the table was my brother? But how could he be? Unless he had been born on a halfshell, like me.

Or not *born* at all. Not from that tiny uterus. Not born, ever.

Like me.

"So now you know," whispered a voice in my ear.

Hasagawa's voice. I could feel him over my shoulder, standing close enough to warm me with his body heat, but not touching.

"Show me the lab," I demanded.

At first I thought he would refuse. But he took me straight there, up three floors and past a door that was unmistakably top security. He had to give his override code three times to get it to let me through.

We passed another room full of technicians and monitors. They didn't look up.

The secret lab looked a lot like the one I had awakened in, except there were more tanks. I wouldn't have called them *re*-generation tanks, though. I would have dropped the prefix. There were about twenty tanks, and each held an occupant in different stages of development. I saw another man with hooves, and a blue-green woman with a serpentine tail instead of legs.

"Your brothers and sisters," remarked Hasagawa. "Beautiful, aren't they? All bought and paid for."

"Did she ever give birth to anyone?" I wondered. "With her own body?"

"I don't know. I've only known her sixty years, and she's always been as she is now."

"How long does it take to grow them?"

He touched the tank with the mermaid-woman in it, lovingly. "Originally it took us about six years. Now we can do it in two. But that's not even our biggest advance. We've been perfecting it all these years. It's staggering, really—it could replace conventional education someday . . ."

"What are you talking about?" I said, more impatiently than I had intended. But he only smiled. "The programming virus."

They've spread throughout your lymph system, said that long-ago doctor, running a hand through his thinning hair. *Almost every gland in your body is infected.*

"And now you know everything I know."

"I doubt that." I made myself look away from my brothers and sisters, into Hasagawa's perfect face. "For instance, I don't know why I was sent to Earth."

"You weren't good enough."

"Excuse me?"

"Don't take it personally." He looked at the vats again, and his eyes actually shone. "See how fabulous they are? How fantastical? You were quite an accomplishment at the time, a perfect *Homo sapiens*. She modeled you after some woman from the Tharsis region as I recall . . ."

I tried to laugh, but I couldn't catch my breath. "I was too ordinary?"

"You were just the prototype. You didn't even get a very good programming virus. There were inconsistencies—"

"At least I got the right job."

"I suppose. But you *worked* with a Machine. These *are* the Machines."

"Really. And they won't have anything to say about that?"

"Of course they will. They'll say, 'I want you.'" He checked his chronometer and frowned. "We'd better get out of here. They'll be just about through their second climax now."

I followed him, but I couldn't help throwing a look over my shoulder at the people in the tanks. The dim lights in the lab made their faces eerily beautiful. I wondered what it would be like to make love to one of them.

"So this is the cutting edge," I said, as the security door sealed behind us.

"Oh, no." Hasagawa gave me the ghost of a smile. "That's in another lab."

But he didn't tell me what it was, and I didn't ask.

Bette Rodriguez's operation went perfectly. I watched the entire procedure and was surprised at my own lack of queasiness. It turned out to be just another piece of art.

Or perhaps I'm not giving Hasagawa his due. He cut and shaped her flesh, used tiny bioimplants, manipulated bone and muscle with a control of his medium that would make the great artists of the past weep with envy. The experience was moving, and when it was over I thanked him.

"Your work is excellent, doctor." I gave him a small bow, to show my gratitude on Bette's behalf. I hoped he would find it an appropriate gesture.

"Thank you," he said, managing to suggest Japanese humility without actually having to display it.

From there, Bette was moved to a regeneration tank, which would heal her incisions without the trace of a scar. I visited her every day, studying her sleeping face for any signs of imperfection. But she remained beautiful, and her skin healed perfectly.

When Bette woke up five days later, she didn't even have any swelling. I was there to greet her.

"How did it go?" she asked sleepily. "Is it all right?"

"It's perfect," I said. "Go look in the mirror."

She dashed into the mirrored bathroom. When fifteen minutes had passed and she hadn't returned, I began to wonder if she would turn out to be one of those people who could never recognize beauty in her own face. But a moment later she emerged smiling.

"Thank you," she said.

"You're welcome." I smiled back, surprised at my own pleasure in her happiness. This new job was giving me a feeling of satisfaction I had never felt during my video years. I wanted to keep doing it.

After Bette was dry and dressed again, I escorted her into the big lobby outside the hospital building, where other, much richer clients sat in elegant chairs, sipping beverages and pretending not to wonder what everyone else was there for. Bette was so happy she didn't even notice the calculating stares.

"I can't wait to show the world my new face," she said as she waved to me and turned to march confidently out the big double doors. She was young and happy, just starting her new life.

"Lysel!" Mother was calling me from across the lobby. I turned my back on the sight of Bette's freedom and went to greet the woman who had made me.

"Twenty clients have requested you for next week alone," she said without preamble. "I've canceled your office in town and cleared those other clients from your schedule. You've proven you can handle the first-rate jobs."

She was smiling at me, but I didn't react. Four of my clients had just been kissed off without an explanation, and I had *liked* my office.

"Any other orders?" I asked.

She turned on her heel, tossing her hair in my general direction as she laughed at me over her shoulder. "As long as you keep doing good work," she said.

I walked back to the main building, so numb that I hardly felt the augmented sunshine on my face. The sand storms had ended only the night before, and already the vacuum men had sucked the place clean. I could hear their blowers out in the street, like the distant drone of bees.

The smell of flowers drifted on the air.

The world was beautiful. Even naked, Mars would have been so. I wished I could have it to myself, just me flying over the Valles Marineris, feasting my eyes on its depth and breadth and length.

Just me and Rico.

As soon as I thought that, Joe's face popped into my mind. I knew it was him by the electrical glitter to his eyes. *Forgotten me already*, querida? he wondered. *Don't you want to know what happened to me?*

But I didn't want to know. Because if I found out, I might just find little Mother and squeeze her throat until her eyes bugged out. I wanted to do that right now, but common sense was holding me back. I couldn't be the only person who wanted Mother dead, and certainly not the most powerful; yet she was still alive. If I found out how callously she had dispatched Joe and Ann, I might forget to be smart.

The flowers teased my nose again. What season was it, anyway? We were somewhere near the equator, but I wasn't sure just what that meant on Mars. With the weather dome in place, the seasons might not vary there too much. Yet here were those flowers, acting as if today were the first day of spring. I hadn't smelled anything quite like them on Earth, so they must have been Mars hybrids.

I didn't go into the main building. Instead, I went around the side, in search of the flowers.

The main building was a simple but elegant thing, soaring above me in the low gravity to a height that would have been envied by those frustrated builders of Notre Dame. I had never walked around it before, or anywhere else in the compound, for that matter, since I'd been sure that I would be stopped and told to go back to my room. Now I was surprised to find a wall, over which hung flowering vines. At the joint of wall and building I found my first security gate. It was twenty feet high, and it was locked.

The sight of it really pissed me off.

This was one retinal lock that wasn't going to let me in, that was for sure, but I still intended to get past it. I wanted to see those damned flowers. I couldn't live my own life or go to my own bloody office, but I was going to look at the flowers. The wall was too smooth to climb, and I couldn't jump more than a little over halfway up, despite the low gravity; otherwise I would have given it a go right then and there. So how else could I do it?

I looked around as I thought. I looked out over the canyon and saw a flier. He glided with apparent ease out of sight. I smiled and made my plans.

The man at the rent-a-flier was eager to teach me how to use a glider. He harnessed me into it himself, double-checking the straps around my torso and smiling at me with perfect teeth, making sure I got the best look possible at his ruggedly handsome face.

"You're in great shape," he said. "You breezed

through the simulator twice as fast as most people do."

"Thank you," I said, very pleased with myself and my crazy plan. I even enjoyed his attention. I had never done *that* before, either.

"*But*," he continued, "don't get the idea that these things aren't dangerous. I want you to fly over the safety zone the first few times. See the nets?" He pointed over the edge of the launching platform, into the abyss.

"Yes." The nets hung a few hundred feet below us. I almost expected to see clumsy fliers stuck there like bugs in a spider's web, but they were empty. That was encouraging.

"Are you scared?" he asked professionally.

"No."

"I'm supposed to tell you that you should be, but I'll skip that one with you. I think you'll do better than most. But I'm ready to come after you if you get into trouble, okay?"

"Okay."

"Don't let the height get to you. Remember, you have wings."

"I will," I said.

He stood back. I took the running steps I had mastered in the training session and launched myself out over the canyon without the slightest trepidation.

The gulf opened beneath my feet, and the harness tightened slightly around my body. I felt the wind catch my wings and hold them as I flew out over the nets. It felt good. It felt so good that it almost made everything else worthwhile.

I tried some experimental turns, wide ones at first, then tighter ones as I got the feel of the wind. There were unexpected gusts as I encountered thermals, but I learned to compensate for them, to go up when I wanted up and down when I wanted down without wobbling and panicking. I worked until my muscles were humming and I was ready to leave the nest.

I could see my instructor on the platform, watching me. I waved at him and signaled my intention. He gave me the go-ahead wave, and I went.

I was laughing as I floated over the central rift, toward Mother's house. This was outrageous, insane. I had no idea whether there would be any place in that garden for me to land, whether there might be guards with force guns in hidden posts, waiting to shoot down aerial assaults of the sort I was about to make. But I didn't care.

The house was about ten miles away, a tiny little measurement in that vast canyon system. If I had wanted to fly to one of the other ridges, it would have taken me most of the day. My instructor had bragged that he did that from time to time, taking catnaps in the glider when he got tired, but I was glad I had only a short way to go. Just the same, it took me an hour to get there.

I flew past Mother's terrace. Fortunately, she wasn't there, but I saw Rashad in an outdoor gymnasium on my way over the roof. He was suspended between two parallel rings, concentrating on a perfect acrobatic maneuver. I didn't think he saw me.

Finally the garden swung into view, and I executed some short turns while I scouted a landing place. There were flowers, shrubs, trees, rows of densely growing vegetables, but not one clear space for landing. I wondered if I should try for the rooftop, but I didn't want to risk alerting Rashad. My loops were getting smaller and smaller, and I was losing altitude, but I stubbornly wouldn't give up my plan.

A sudden change in the wind made my decision for me. It dropped me right onto the top of the wall, and I seized the moment, instantly folding the wings as I had been taught in the training session. I perched on the top of the wall like a bird and undid my harness.

I secured the wings to the top of the wall and opened my utility pouch. I had bought it and its contents in a climber's supply store on the way to the rent-a-flier, in the event that I might have to climb down from the roof. I pulled out a hooked rope ladder and secured it to the wall, letting the ladder dangle down the vine-covered surface.

Climbing down in that gravity was easy. In fact, I was beginning to wonder if I was being weakened by Mars's light touch. But I didn't let the notion dampen my mood. I stepped into the garden and tiptoed down a narrow path, feeling very pleased with my conquest.

Someone loved this garden. It was densely grown, but there were no weeds, no neglected flowers rotting under heavy ferns and choking vines. The blooms were lush, their colors complemented by the sunset light rather than overwhelmed by it, and their perfumes didn't clash, as if the gardener had been as conscious of their scents as he had been of their colors and growing habits when he chose to put them there.

Or she. But I hoped it wasn't Mother's garden. I didn't want to imagine her taking pleasure in this beauty.

The path took a turn into a tiny glade, and I saw

the gardener bending over a small row of yellow blooms, gently weeding the rich soil beneath them, his giant hands tenderly touching their stalks as he inspected them for marauding insects. His long black hair was tied at the nape of his neck, but other than that, the red demon was naked, as always.

He froze suddenly and turned his head in my direction. I poised to run, but I waited to see what he would do first. He saw me, but he remained absolutely motionless, not even moving his hands from the flowers.

"You," he said softly, "from the hallway."

"Please don't chase me," I said. "I'll only run away."

"Then why are you here?" His beautiful face was clouded with conflicting emotions, but he was trying to control them. I was sure of it.

"I wanted to see this beautiful garden."

He smiled, his face lighting up like the sun. "It's *my* garden," he said proudly. "I like to make things grow."

"You're gifted. Have you always liked flowers?"

"From the beginning."

I wondered if he had been specifically programmed for it, or if the gardening talent was just an interesting fluke.

"What's your name?" I asked.

"Devil."

He said it so innocently, so trustingly, it made me feel very angry with Mother. She could have given him a name. Calling him "Devil" was like naming me "Whore."

"My name is Lucy."

"Lucy." He moved, very carefully, until he was

kneeling, facing me. His penis was hard, and it made me think of the stamens that were nodding from the blooms on the nearby bushes. "Do you want me, Lucy?" he asked, and his voice was like rich, warm honey, pooling between my legs and heating me all the way up my spine. But I answered carefully. After all, Mother had felt it necessary to tie his wrists and ankles. Maybe he didn't know his own strength.

"I want to be your friend. Do you understand what I mean?"

"Yes," he said. "Sometimes I feel very lonely. But I'm dangerous."

"How are you dangerous?"

"I've killed," he said, with considerable shame. "A man. I was jealous."

"I see." I had to stifle the urge to get up and run. His confession frightened me. To imagine a being that size being angry with me, attacking me . . .

"My sister killed all the time," he said, as if reading my mind. "She was made wrong. But she loved me, and Mother was jealous. Mother punished us when we—once, we—"

"You don't have to tell me. I understand."

"She sent my sister away, to Earth, and I'll never see her again."

"To Earth?"

"That's where Mother sends her mistakes."

Anger flared in my chest again, but this time for the sake of Devil's sister. "Did your sister look like you?"

"She was white instead of red. Mother named her Scorpianne."

For a long moment I didn't believe him. But then the truth seemed obvious. The hooves on the floor, just like his, going CLUNK CLUNK CLUNK. Mother's mistake on the loose, doing what came naturally for her.

"I used to think Mother was Scorpianne," I confided.

"Why?" he said, looking utterly astonished at the notion. I wondered how I could possibly begin to explain when suddenly the simplicity of the situation occurred to me.

"Because Scorpianne wanted to kill me."

"Oh, yes," he said. "Scorpianne will kill you if she can. But I hope she doesn't. I hope—"

His molten eyes pleaded with mine. "I want you," he said. "I'm working very hard to control myself."

"Is it so hard?"

"Yes. But—" he lowered his voice and looked around the garden, a frightened expression passing over his face like a shadow. "It's getting easier," he whispered. "A little."

"You practice?" I whispered back. "Resisting, I mean?"

"Yes. It—hurts to always want—and not be able—" He broke off, looking about the garden as if he could find the illusive words there.

"I know what you mean," I said.

He smiled again. "But I wish I could have you, Lucy. You're like—" again he looked at his garden, and this time he found a flower to show me. "You're like this. Ripe and round here and here, slender and delicate there and there." His hand caressed the petals that managed to stay a soft pink, despite the Martian light.

I wanted him. His scent must have been mingling

with the flowers. Before too long, I would have to leave, or I would do something stupid.

"I think you want me too," he said. "I can smell you."

"Don't chase me," I warned gently. "I *do* want you, but I want something else even more."

"What?" he asked eagerly.

"Your friendship."

"Friendship more than love?"

"Sometimes love is bad for you."

"Yes," he agreed. "I know."

I knelt on the grass myself, to show him my sincerity. He quivered when he saw me move, but he continued to hold himself in check. "May I call you by another name?" I asked him. "A between-friends kind of name?"

"What will you call me?"

Actually I hadn't had anything particular in mind, I just didn't want to call him Devil. But I didn't want to stick him with something haphazard either, something meaningless. "Do you know a name you like very much?" I asked him.

"I like John," he said without hesitation. "Do you like that name?"

"Yes," I said, though I was amused to think of how many johns I had known in my life.

"I've been reading the John Carter books," he said. "*A Princess of Mars, The Chessmen of Mars*—I like the hero very much. He's brave and clever, and he loves a woman with red skin, like mine."

He ran a hand sensually over his skin, and my heart began to pound.

"Then I'll call you John Carter," I said. "Everyone

should have a first and last name. Mine is Lucy
Cartier."

"*Car*-tee-ay. Why do you want to be my friend,
Lucy?" He stroked the pink blossom and turned his
face away from mine, so I couldn't tell if he thought
it was good I would rather be his friend or bad I
wouldn't be his lover.

"You and I came from the same place, John."

"The tank?" he whispered, still without looking.

"Yes."

"But you didn't live here before. I would have
smelled you. Where have you been?" He looked up
at me again, with a startled expression. "Were you
on Earth?"

"Yes."

"Of course, with Scorpianne! I want to go to Earth
too. I want to have adventures like John Carter. And
I want to see what the rest of Mars is like."

"What about Mother?"

"I want her."

"You want her to go with you?"

"No. I just want her."

"Oh. I think I understand." His face was turning
rather sad, so I decided to change the subject. "Do
you like math?"

He frowned. "Yes—"

"How much is six times one hundred?"

"Six hundred."

"What is forty-two divided by seven?"

"Six. Why are you asking me those simple things?
Are you trying to find out if I'm stupid?"

"No. I'm trying to find out if you're smart. Obviously you are."

He lowered his voice again. "Why wouldn't I be?"

I wondered if I was really doing him any favors by telling him. But he was intelligent, he deserved answers. "I wanted to find out if you had been made for only one thing."

"Oh." He understood immediately. "If I had no intelligence, I would just be an animal. Animals are not good lovers."

"Lots of people aren't either."

He laughed. His hands had been rubbing his lower legs, and his smile faded a little when he touched the hooves that grew where his feet should have been. "I've wondered something," he said. "I don't understand why she gave me *these* instead of feet."

"She wanted you to look like a fertility god. From Earth."

He nodded. "But they aren't as good as feet. It's harder to balance, and sometimes I get terrible cramps in my calves. I have to rub them until they go away, but sometimes—I wish someone else would rub them for me. Just to make me feel . . ."

"I wish I could do that for you, John, really I do." In fact, I wished it so much, I knew that if I didn't leave within the next five minutes I would be over there rubbing his calves, kissing his skin, hugging and holding him.

"Please do," he said, struggling to be polite.

I made myself do the right thing. "I have to leave in a minute, John, but I want to ask you one more question."

"What, Lucy?"

"Do you love yourself?"

I had expected him to answer quickly, like he had answered my other questions. But he was stumped.

"What?" he asked.

"Do you love yourself? Think about how you love Mother, how you feel about me, and apply it to yourself."

"You mean do I touch myself?" He stroked his penis, which pretty much answered that question, but it wasn't what I had meant.

"No, I'm talking about good feelings. You're handsome, smart, a talented gardener . . ."

"I like it when people tell me those things."

"But do you tell them to yourself?"

He shook his head. "Should I?"

"Yes. And believe them. Look in the mirror and see how beautiful you are; but more important, look *inside* yourself, John. Your spirit is beautiful too. When you're working in your garden, you're most beautiful of all. Understand?"

"I'm not sure." He touched himself again, obviously enjoying the sensation. "I like the way this feels. I like to make myself—happy."

"Keep making yourself happy. When Mother is mean to you, don't believe that it's all your fault, John."

He lowered his head. "I know what you're talking about. But I don't think I'd better tell Mother so."

"I don't think so either. Listen, I'd better go."

He nodded. I thought he might cry, so I stood quickly. "I like you, John. And I like your wonderful garden."

He didn't look up. "Will you come again?"

"I hope I can. But you know Mother."

"Yes," he said. "I know."

I turned and left, trying not to hurry. I didn't want to trigger some chasing instinct he might have, and I also didn't want to hurt his feelings. I went to my rope ladder and started to climb, trying to concentrate on the task at hand and clear my head. I was about six feet up when a giant hand closed around my ankle, holding me firmly in place. I gasped and looked down.

John was looking up at me. Tears streaked his face, but he looked hopeful. "If you can live outside, perhaps I can too, someday," he said.

"Would you like that?" I tried not to look scared. Or aroused.

"Yes," he said, and let go of my ankle. "I've been practicing. See? I'm getting better."

"Yes," I agreed. "You are. Just remember what I said, okay?"

"I will," he said, and took a step back. Only then did I begin my climb again.

I repacked the ladder. When I had put it away again I glanced down at John and suddenly felt very guilty for not asking him to climb it as well. But he hadn't even tried. He knew perfectly well that he wasn't ready. That took more than intelligence, as far as I was concerned. I smiled at him and struggled back into my wings.

"Don't fall," he called.

"I won't." Actually I wasn't sure about that.

"Someday I'd like to fly, too."

"It's good to make plans. But it's good not to talk about them to the wrong people."

"Good luck," he said.

I waved and swooped down off the wall.

It didn't prove to be such a great idea. I had enough lift to fly, but I was gliding too low, and I had to run like mad as I hit the ground. I almost stumbled and fell flat on my face, just barely managing to keep my legs under me and slow down, then fold the wings again. I was breathing hard, but I had survived my own recklessness. I was laughing as I struggled out of the wings again, turning the corner without looking where I was going.

I ran smack into Rashad.

"Was that you I saw flying over the house?" he demanded.

I almost lost my smile, but years of practice kept it in place. "Yes," I laughed again. "I almost killed myself! I got all screwed up and ended up over the buildings. You should have seen my *landing*!"

He was almost smiling by then, but I saw his eyes dart in the direction of the garden.

"You must have seen me on the roof then," he said.

"Yes. I didn't know there was a gym up there. And whose garden is that, anyway? It looks kind of overgrown."

"That belongs to her," he said, and he didn't need to say who she was. "You'd better stay away from it. It's her private place."

"Oh." I put a mildly disappointed look on my face. "Okay. Well, I'd better get this back."

"Do you need a ride?" He moved closer, as if testing to see if I was feeling any more amorous than I had been before. I pretended not to notice.

"No, I need the walk. This gravity is turning me into a weakling."

"I know what you mean." He flexed a beautiful bicep. "I have to work out several times a day. I'm working on a new virus though, one with interesting possibilities." He winked at me. "I'll let you know how it goes. Then maybe we'll have more quality time to spend together."

"No time," I sighed. "The bane of modern existence." I was already walking away by then, waving to him. He waved back and seemed convinced.

I congratulated myself again.

I returned to the house late in the evening. My instructor had asked me out to supper, but I had begged off, pleading late work at my office. I was still a good enough actress to make him feel that I liked him and found him interesting, which was true, though I didn't plan to pursue it. He didn't need to have his life ruined just because I was feeling flirtatious.

I had supper in my own room, going over my new case files. I was surprised to find the Finklesteins and Red Hulot in there. I was staring at their faces and wondering what the hell I was going to do with them when Mother suddenly threw open my door. I jumped like a cat.

"Lysel," she cried, all smiles. "I'm glad to see you've been looking at those files. The Finklesteins are here now, and they'd like to talk to you. Are you ready?"

"Yes," I said, relieved to see her good mood. "How about right here?"

"Perfect. They can see your fine taste in art as well. That'll boost their confidence."

She ran off to fetch them, and I went to look at my bar. Would they want alcohol? I couldn't remember what they had said about that, if anything.

"I hope she wasn't sleeping!" I heard Lisa Finklestein's voice coming down the hall, and she sounded more insulted by the idea of my lying in bed when there was work to be done than dismayed by the possibility of disturbing me. The three of them came bursting through the door together, and I turned to face them. I smiled gently at the Finklesteins. Meyer smiled back.

"At least you've got good taste in art," said Lisa, going immediately to study the work that hung on the walls and stood on the tables.

"I'm glad you like it," I said. "Would you like something to drink?"

"Vodka and tonic for me," said Meyer. "I always need one when I talk serious business."

Lisa didn't speak up, but Mother said, "Rum and Coke for me, dear," and plopped herself down on the couch where she could see the monitor.

I made the drinks, glad that at least they had wanted something I had been used to preparing for myself after a hard day on the Machine. Meyer sat near Mother, but Lisa was still wandering among the pieces of art.

I gave Meyer and Mother their drinks and sat down near the monitor controls. "I'm glad you're here," I told Meyer. "I had just been looking at your files when Mother came in. I could see a number of possibilities, but they depend very much on your attitude. This could go in several directions—"

"Show me some." Meyer gestured toward the screen with his drink. It sloshed a little, and I wondered how many he had drunk before this one.

"Well, okay." I made some changes in his image on the screen as I spoke. "I've noticed that you seem fond of the Mongolian look, and your previous sculptor did a good job carrying that off, if that's what you wanted . . ."

"Um-hum," said Meyer noncommittally.

"If you like it, we can make subtle changes that will make it impossible for real Mongolians to tell you're not one of them. Except for your dark skin, of course. Like so."

"Uh-huh . . ."

"Or we could go for more of a blend of Asian and Eastern European. The Siberians are quite handsome people, and the Amur are too. Their features would go quite well with your skin color."

"I see," said Meyer.

I continued to make subtle changes, all of them turning Meyer into a striking man of an entirely different race than the one he'd been born to. I found myself wondering what he had looked like originally. Had he been short and fat? With a nose he hated and red cheeks? But no one was fat anymore, not even the very poor.

"Mind if I look at your stuff in the bedroom?" called Lisa.

"Not at all," I called back.

"Oh, Lisa!" Mother jumped up to join her. "Let me show you something!" The two of them disappeared, shutting the door behind them.

I continued to fiddle with the monitor, talking to Meyer as I did so and getting "um-hums" out of him, until finally I felt his eyes on me. I looked up, and he smiled.

"I don't share my wife's taste in figures," he said.

"Really?" He was as handsome as Rashad, but I leaned away from him, as if I were trying to get more comfortable. I drew my legs up and folded them to the side, maintaining my neutral position. "Are you disappointed with the outcome of your wife's makeover?"

"Not at all," he said. "I think she's exquisite. It's been quite a help to our marriage, let me tell you." He winked.

"I'm glad to hear that."

"It's just that the sight of you drives me wild." He let his eyes wander up and down my body. "And the knowledge that you were a high-priced whore drives me even wilder."

"That's interesting. But will it interfere with your judgment concerning my work as your sculptor? Perhaps you ought to work with someone else."

"No." He smiled. "I can see you know what you're doing. In fact, I'm disappointed."

"Disappointed?"

"She promised me first bid on you when you arrived."

"Excuse me?"

His smiled widened, and he leaned toward me. "I know where you're from, sweetheart. And I know what you're for."

"Is that so?"

"She asked me to come to the cafe so I could see you. You really knocked my eyes out. Who knew you were going to turn out to be the best face sculptor on Mars?"

"Yes, that must have been a surprise."

"You can earn more in a year than I could pay for you in my lifetime." He shrugged. "Too bad. Because right now I'm imagining you with your legs tied open and your arms manacled to a bedpost. I'd like to see if that hot cunt of yours is as pink as your mouth."

"Meyer!" Lisa came bounding out of my bedroom, her face flushing a deeper green with excitement. "She's got an Ernst in here! A Max Ernst!"

"Lisa loves the Surrealists," Meyer said affectionately.

"Lovely," I said, as numbness crept from the top of my head all the way down to my toes.

"Let's see that Siberian look again," said Meyer, as if our other conversation had never taken place.

I did as he asked, and Lisa came over to see. "God, that's sexy," she said when I had finished. "Oh, Meyer, I like that."

"I like it too," he said. "Make a copy of that for me, Lysel. I'd like to take it home and put it up where I can study it."

"All right."

"Make one for me, too," commanded Lisa.

"Let's see what she can do for you, darling," Meyer moved over on the couch and patted the spot next to him. She sat gracefully and fixed her eyes on the screen. I dialed up her image.

"Here you are with a more Chinese face," I said, and put in the missing folds on her eyelids. I made some minor changes in her brows and mouth too, and heard a gasp from her. "I didn't think my face could get any better," she said. But then she added, "What else can you do?"

I did the same for her as I had done for Meyer, showing her a variety of Asian and Eastern European faces. In the end she wanted three different copies to study. I could see she was going to be tough, possibly dissatisfied no matter what the outcome was. But she smiled when I was finished.

"You're worth your weight in gold, you know that?"

"She certainly is." Meyer licked his lips suggestively, but I think his tone fooled Lisa. "We'll take these home with us and get back in touch with you when we've had a chance to get a feel for them."

"Right," I said, as the two of them stood. Mother still lurked in the bedroom.

"Good-bye," Lisa called.

"Good-bye," came Mother's muffled voice.

"Good-bye," I said, and showed them to the door.

When they were gone, I went into the bedroom. Mother was standing there, in front of the Ernst, her drink dangling from one hand. She didn't look at me when I came in. My face was so stiff with hate, I could barely shape it into the blankness I knew might save my life.

"You're right about them," I said. "They're tough customers."

"They're creeps," said Mother. "But Lisa is right about this painting. It's fascinating. Isn't it odd how this figure looks so human, yet inhuman at the same time? You want to find the familiar lines, but they're not there."

"Yes," I said.

"And its skin seems to be coming off. Peeling off, like wallpaper."

"I hadn't noticed that."

"You will. Especially if you ever bother Devil again."

I didn't speak. It would have been pointless.

"If you ever go near him or talk to him again, I'll

have your skin peeled off in strips, Lysel. And I'll make sure nothing grows in its place. Understand?"

"I think so."

She looked at me and smiled like an angel. "I'm glad. For a while there I was beginning to wonder if I had wasted my time telling Machine Co. not to dispose of you. I brought you back here on a whim, Lysel, out of curiosity, but I won't let you touch what's mine."

"Not even myself?" I asked.

She laughed. "That's very clever. Now go to bed, dear. You have lots of work to do tomorrow."

She strolled past me, her every movement confident and completely self-satisfied. As she went past me my hands ached to fasten around her throat, but I held myself back, warned by intuition. I glanced down and saw something metallic flashing in her palm. I wondered what it was. But she was past me before I could get a better look at it.

"Red Hulot wants to see you, too," she said. "God knows what you're going to do with *him*."

As she slammed the door behind her, I wondered what Red Hulot thought he was going to do with *me*. I was a little sad at the thought. He had seemed like an honest man, considering that he was a billionaire. I didn't really want to hear him saying the same things Meyer had said.

I was so tired by then, I barely had the energy to strip down to my underwear before I fell into bed. I thought briefly about my talk with John, trying to savor the sight and smell of him in my memory. But I was asleep before I could focus on him properly, and it was Rico who came into my dreams.

I know where you're from, baby, he said, *and I know what you're for.*

"Rico," I said.

A hand clamped down over my mouth, and my eyes flew open. Someone strong was standing over me. Someone male. He was pressing me down into the bed with his body, fumbling with something in his right hand. A familiar smell filled my nostrils, somebody's personal scent. Then a sharp pain stabbed my arm, and I felt a rush of energy. It was immediately followed by a leaden numbness, and my eyes drooped.

He began to wrap me in a blanket.

"Who—?" I mumbled.

"Be quiet," hissed Rico. He lifted me in his arms, and I fell into a nice warm nothingness.

woke up very slowly, and the first thing I was aware of was movement. I was lying on a flat surface, inside some kind of vehicle. The wind howled outside, which was disorienting, because it made me think it was weeks before, back during the dust storm. But then I remembered what had happened since, everything flooding back in a sort of panic, and I tried to move. That's when I discovered I was tied up.

By the time the vehicle came to a halt, I was wide awake. I think it must have been several hours later, maybe as much as a day. I was tied inside a blanket, but I could feel a chill creeping into the vehicle. The compartment I was in was perhaps eight feet long by six wide, four feet from floor to ceiling. When we came to a stop I lay there tensely, waiting to see what would happen next.

A panel slid open, and Rico pulled himself through. He was wearing a plain black flight suit. He immediately checked to see if I was awake, and I saw no reason to pretend that I wasn't. He pulled the panel shut behind him and crab-walked over to some lockers against one wall.

"Are you hungry?" he asked.

"Yes." I watched him for some sign of his mood. He looked very tired. He pulled out some bars wrapped in cellophane and a thermos and brought them to me. He propped me up against the wall and began to unwrap a bar.

"You're not going to untie me?" I asked.

"No."

"Why?"

His jaw muscles jumped, and he looked away from me while he took some deep breaths. His anger was so palpable, I began to be frightened.

Finally he returned to unwrapping the bar. He held it to my mouth and watched me eat. He was very careful, giving me small sips of the water so I wouldn't choke or spill it, brushing away any crumbs that fell on my blanket. He worked at it as if it were an important and absorbing task. It wasn't until I was almost finished eating that he ventured to look into my eyes.

He looked away quickly, but then he looked back again, and this time he lingered.

"You're scared," he said.

"Yes."

"I like seeing you that way."

"I'm glad you're enjoying yourself."

The tension between us was growing with every passing moment. I wasn't sure if he wanted to kiss me or beat me senseless. He was just sitting there, motionless, staring.

"How did you get into the complex?" I asked him.

"I walked in."

"You don't think they saw you?"

"I know they didn't. My communications buddy scoped out their defenses. They rely on reputation to keep people out of the living quarters, and harder stuff for the labs."

"Mother would have more than reputation to protect her own quarters."

He laughed harshly. "She does. My buddy Chavez fell into a rock pulverizer."

I couldn't quite grasp it. I had never seen his buddy, never heard his name, and now I had trouble visualizing the reality of his death. The only way I could really believe it was to look into Rico's eyes. He had seen what he was telling.

"Who pushed him?" I asked.

"Someone inside the service." His eyes were watching mine so intently that they almost twitched, and small veins stood out on his temples. Suddenly he seized my chin and leaned over me threateningly. "He was hamburger when he came out of that machine, Lucy. And I heard him screaming. He screamed for a lot longer than you would think."

His anguish was catching. I was beginning to be able to imagine how he was feeling, and I didn't want to.

"Look at you," he said. "You really look horrified. You really look like you're surprised to hear about it."

I didn't try to protest my innocence. "What did your buddy find out?" I asked him.

"Why?" he squeezed my chin painfully. "You want to know how far the damage has spread so you can report back to your boss?"

It was difficult to speak with a vice on my jaw, but I did anyway. "I don't have a boss anymore. Now that she knows I'm with you, she'll kill us both."

"I hope I get to watch you go first," he said, but I could see that was a lie. He wanted something from me. He wanted reassurance.

"Please tell me," I said softly. "You tell me what you found out, and I'll tell you what I found out."

"You first."

So I told him. I started with the day my Machine knifed me in the butt and ended with Mother's last conversation. While I talked, he backed off a little. He let go of my chin, and his posture became less rigid.

Finally he said, "You came out of a tank?"

"Yes."

"That's why you're so beautiful."

I had to smile. "No. When I first went to Earth, I was just attractive. I made *myself* beautiful. I did it for my business."

He nodded. I could see the thoughts swirling around in his head like wild birds.

"Now it's your turn," I said.

But he was shaking his head. "It's crazy," he said. "I looked at you that day in the cafe, and I wanted you. I was willing to go to any length to get you, especially after the way you kissed me. After what you said about how I remind you of that guy. Joe. I couldn't think about anything else, day and night. And this is where it gets me."

"Yes," I said.

"I'm out of the service. They've got me up on charges. But I won't make it to trial."

"Then where are we going? You must have a plan."

"I do. I'm not gonna die like Chavez did, and neither are you."

"So what did Chavez find out that got him killed?"

"Shit." He dropped his face in his hands and scrubbed at it like he wanted to wipe the memory right out. I thought he would be crying when he looked up again, but his eyes were dry. "For the past month he's been—he was trying to find out how far the connection went between Designer Gene Co. and the force. Turned out it goes as far as it can. Four top admirals and two generals are involved in the program. The System president too."

"The *program*?"

"Just think about it for a minute, Lucy. You've been living sex so long, you think that's all that's going on."

"So enlighten me."

"People are always trying to come up with ways to make a better soldier. Human error, discipline problems, fatigue, physical limitations—when it comes down to the bottom line, they want to know the best way to get the job done. Now throw in some generating tanks, only they're not growing sexy red men in them."

For some reason I thought of Scorpianne. Why had she really been grown? For love, or for war?

"So they're trying to make better men," I said.

"Not even that. Men have limitations, Lucy. We're not built right. What they're planning to make doesn't look anything like *me*. It doesn't even have the same number of legs. It doesn't have a gender, a sex drive. It doesn't feel regret when it kills."

He was getting mad while he talked about it. I hadn't realized before just how dedicated Rico was to the service, to honor. "What kind of war would they fight with that?" I asked him humbly.

"No kind of war. They wouldn't have to. They

could just send their killing machines in to tidy up any annoying uprisings. Anywhere."

"Sooner or later another company would design the same thing, Rico—"

"Not if their best minds are dead. Pretty soon they will be."

That gave me a clue about where we might be going. But I kept silent. He wasn't looking at me anymore, he was staring off into space. He looked very determined and very worried.

Outside the wind howled louder.

"Where are we?" I ventured.

"Going north."

"Will you untie me?" I asked.

"No."

"Why not?"

He didn't answer.

"Rico—"

He picked up his food bar and began to eat it.

"I have to urinate."

He looked at me, startled, and I almost laughed. He hadn't thought of that. But he got himself under control quickly. He crawled over to me and began to untie me.

"It's one hundred below zero out there," he warned me. "You won't get far in your underwear if you try to run. We're about three hundred kilometers out from under the weather dome."

"All right." I rubbed my arms and legs as the ropes and blanket came free. I wasn't trying to be seductive, but it had a visible effect on him. He tried to ignore it.

"The toilet is back here," he said, and went to the panel he had originally come through. He pulled it open and reached into the left side of the small compartment on the other side. He pulled open a smaller panel and thumbed on a light.

I crouched down and made my way awkwardly to the opening. He tried not to watch me, but he couldn't seem to help himself. I crawled through and found the little toilet. I almost went then and there, but I remembered to close the panel at the last moment. I didn't want him to think I was trying to seduce him. He might tie me up again.

When I was done, I crawled awkwardly out again. He was sitting with his back to me, eating. I went back to my blanket and wrapped myself in it.

"Do you have any clothes for me?" I asked him.

"You can stay in your underwear for the time being. You won't get far that way."

"I'm not going to run away, Rico. I'm glad you came and got me."

It was true. Mother had been killing me slowly with her threats and her manipulations. I was so happy to be away from her—happy to be alone with Rico. John had been tempting, but I couldn't help loving Rico the way I had loved Joe. Especially now, when he seemed more like Joe than ever.

"I'll go with you wherever you need me to go," I promised him. "I'm not being romantic, Rico. I mean it. You're offering me the best choice I've heard in a long time."

"You don't even know what I'm planning," he said, without looking at me.

"Yes I do. You're going to the orbital colony. To YoungTech. You're going to tell them what you know."

He pulled a small, flat case out of one of his pockets, the kind of case used to store computer information. "I'm going to *show* them," he said. "But first I'm going to spill the information to every major news agency in the system."

I gaped at the case. "Is that—"

"Everything," he said. "Memos, documentation, videos of prototypes. Chavez gave it to me just before he—he said he thought someone was following him, so . . ."

He was breathing harshly, and his face began to redden, crumple. "He gave it to me just five minutes before . . ."

Rico hunched over, sobbing. I was astonished. He had been so intimidating a moment before, and now he was so vulnerable it broke my heart. I felt helpless. He looked at me pleadingly, wanting something very badly. It took me several moments to figure out what it was.

I had never comforted anyone before. I was awkward about it. But I scuttled over to him as quickly as I could. I took him in my arms and held him while he cried with deep, racking sobs. Men cry so seldom, when they finally let it out it seems to tear them apart. I could barely hold on to him.

"We'll tell everyone," I said. "It's time to blow the lid off."

He grabbed me and held me tight, rocking me long into the night with the fury of his anguish.

"How far north are we?" I asked Rico the next morning. I tried not to take it personally when he wouldn't answer.

At least I was allowed to ride up front with him, though I still wasn't allowed clothing. I wrapped myself in the blanket, more for warmth than modesty. Outside it was one hundred degrees below zero Fahrenheit; inside it was about forty above.

I knew we had to be going north, across the Tharsis shield. The terrain was volcanic, not cratered, as the southern region was supposed to be. But that was just a guess for me. So much debris was blowing against our windshield, I could only catch glimpses through it. I didn't even know we weren't on a proper road until Rico suddenly jammed on the brakes. He stared at sensor readouts on his dash for several moments, frowning and scratching his chin.

"What's up?" I asked.

"Rift," he said. He pressed a button and the readout changed to an electronic representation of a chasm, not five meters from our front wheels. Below one hundred meters, the image was estimated at five hundred meters deep.

"Now what?" I asked.

He looked at several more readouts and finally said, "Backtrack three point four kilometers and then go west for about thirty."

So back we went. I paid a lot more attention to what I could see of the landscape than I had previously. The thought of suddenly falling into something deep was very sobering.

We passed through a small valley I was sure we hadn't gone through earlier. It gave us no more than a foot on either side for passage. "What's that growing on the rock face?" I asked Rico, pointing to what looked like purple smudges.

"Purple sticky," he said. "It was introduced to help keep the dust down around here. You can see how well it works."

"Maybe it does work. Maybe things used to be worse."

He shook his head. "It's hard to get an entire planet to behave."

Right now I would settle for getting one man to behave. He seemed to get more depressed the farther north we went. I wondered what his childhood had been like there, but I didn't ask him about it. He probably didn't need to be reminded of it just then.

Finally we stopped again. "Did we get around?" I asked him.

"As far around as we're going to. I'll have to use the portable ramps now."

"The what?"

He was rubbing his chin. When he finally looked at me, his eyes were red with fatigue. "You're going to have to help me," he said.

"Great. Do I get to wear clothes?"

"Come on." He opened the panel that led to the small crawl space between compartments and pulled his long body inside. He hadn't made me precede him—I thought that was a good sign. I followed him, leaving my blanket on the front seat.

Rico pulled open a storage locker and got out a black flight suit very much like the one he was wearing. He handed it to me and watched me while I pulled it on. He seemed less hesitant to look at my body, less concerned about being aroused by the sight.

The flight suit was a little too long in the legs and arms, plus the waist was too big. But Rico helped me roll up my sleeves and cuffs, and I was delighted to discover the insulating properties of the fabric. I was already toasty. I smiled at him. He didn't quite smile back.

"Get ready for a shock," he said. "It's very cold outside." He fastened a utility belt around his waist, then pulled two hoods and breathing masks out of the locker. He tugged mine in place before doing his own, then went to the door and keyed it open.

Mars came howling in.

We climbed out the back of the vehicle and Rico slammed the door shut. He immediately took hold of my arm, but not to keep me from running away. The debris in the air was disorienting, it bounced against my mask and suit in an almost constant stream. It wasn't an unpleasant sensation, actually, it was painless, but it let up enough to give us unobscured vision only every two minutes or so. Rico snapped something onto a loop in the back of my suit and I felt a cord there. It gave me a much greater feeling of security.

He guided me to a ladder on the right side of the back of the vehicle. "Climb to the roof," he said, his voice amplified by a speaker in the mask. "Your ramp is hooked up there. You should be able to feel how it unhooks once you get up there."

I climbed. I caught glimpses of Rico doing the same up his own ladder. Once on the roof, I looked up just in time to catch a gap in the shifting chaos, and I saw the rift ahead of us. It wasn't terribly wide, but I couldn't tell how deep it was.

I was sitting on the ladder. I felt with my hands for the restraints and found them to be very much like the latches on the pop-out windows in the back seats of many taxis, very simple to operate. There were six of them. I undid each one. Rico was sliding his ramp over the back of the roof, letting it lean against the hatch next to his ladder. I did the same. It seemed to me that the ramp felt rather too light to support a heavy vehicle, but perhaps it was made of some engineered material. I hoped so.

Once I had climbed down, Rico said, "Carry your ramp around to the front of the vehicle. I'll meet you there."

I did, feeling my safety cord unwind behind me. I felt ridiculously proud for being allowed to help him. I wondered what it was like to be a space-air pilot, to do interesting and dangerous things.

"Lucy!" Rico called. His voice seemed worried.

"Here!" I called back, and waved at him through another gap. I saw his eyes behind the visor, worried and red. He put a hand on my arm for a moment, squeezing gently through the fabric.

"If you fall into the rift, you'll fall for about fifty feet," he said. "Use your legs to kick away from the face of the rock."

"I'll try not to fall."

"I've fallen twice," he said. "It'll scare the shit out of you. The best thing to do is put one foot in front of the other; move steadily but cautiously. It's when you get overconfident that accidents happen."

"Okay," I promised, and hefted my ramp.

"And don't drop that! Drag it behind you. These are the only two we've got."

He was moving straight forward from the vehicle now, at least as far as I could tell. I copied him, dragging my ramp and going heel-toe, heel-toe, and in another moment the storm blinded me completely. It was a little hard to keep my balance when walking that way, unable to see at all; but I was pretty sure the rift was about ten meters ahead of us, so I counted my steps. When I got to fifteen, my foot came down over the rift, with only two centimeters of my heel to keep me from pitching right in.

"Christ!" I screamed.

"Lucy!"

"I'm okay!" I staggered back from the edge. "I've still got my ramp."

I felt his hand on my leg, then he was feeling the edge of the rift. "I've got half a meter more than you do on my side," he said, then was silent for a long moment, thinking. I crawled over to him and kneeled with my thigh touching his, waiting for directions.

"Let's try it," he said finally. "We're going to hold one end of this thing and extend the other end to the other side. Don't let go of it for one moment. Hold tight until I tell you."

"Okay."

We picked up one end of the ramp and extended it, together. Held that way, it was much heavier and more cumbersome. It seemed like we were holding it out over nothing, but suddenly I felt a jar as it touched the other side. I almost let go, but made myself hold tight until I heard Rico say, "Let go."

I did, my fingers cramping. He was still holding on to it, but in a moment I felt him lean back against me. "We've got less than one centimeter on either side," he said grimly.

"My God. How deep is this thing?"

He leaned forward again, unstrapping something from his utility belt. I heard some beeps.

"Six hundred meters."

One centimeter was not a comforting margin between me and six hundred meters, that was for sure.

Rico was fiddling with something at the end of the ramp, and I saw green lights go on. He pulled a tape measure out of the side and crawled to the end of its reach. "Come over here carefully, Lucy," he warned.

I crawled, and the two of us did the same thing with his ramp we had done with mine. When he had turned those sensors on too, he said, "I want you to walk across this thing."

"What?"

"Don't be afraid. It's steady. I don't want you in the vehicle if it goes over the side."

"What about you?"

"I'm driving."

"No, Rico."

"Let me get you an emergency pack. I'll give you a locator so you can get to the nearest town if you have to."

I argued with him all the way back to the vehicle, but he wasn't listening. He loaded a pack on my back and kept giving me emergency directions, as if I weren't talking at all. Then he led me back to his ramp. "If you fall, remember what I said." He tugged at the cord attached to my loop to make sure it was secure. "Try not to kick the ramp out of place."

"What are you going to do?" I asked, trying to keep the tears out of my voice.

"I'll guide the vehicle across using the computer. It'll line me right up with the ramps," he said, sounding competent and sure of himself. But if he was so sure, why wouldn't he let me ride with him?

"Unhook your line when you get to the other side," he was saying. "Then take five steps to your left and wait for me."

I couldn't even kiss him good-bye. He was gently

nudging me onto the ramp. I heel-toed across the rift, feeling too numb even to be scared. At least it felt steady under my feet. That was one consolation.

When I felt solid ground, I moved to the left and unhooked the line. Then I waited.

I heard the engine, and I started to shake. It came closer through the storm, and in another moment, I glimpsed front bumpers, creeping toward me. I held my breath.

It moved slowly and steadily. In another moment it was sitting right next to me, idling, and the door slid open. Rico jumped out.

"Okay," he said. "Let's get those ramps and get the hell out of here."

Before he could move again, I grabbed him and hugged him as hard as I could. He hugged me back.

"It's all right, baby," he said confidently. "We did it right."

But he didn't let go of me for a long time.

We had to do the ramp thing three more times that day, but we had much better luck with our spacing. He didn't make me get out and wait for him on the other side again. When night fell we ate our evening rations and curled up together in the back of the vehicle. We were both tired, but we couldn't seem to go right to sleep.

"I've been thinking about those generating tanks," Rico said. "All the stuff they could grow in them."

"Yes," I agreed, beginning to think about it myself.

"Like asteroid miners," he said. He propped his arms behind his head and stared up at the dim ceiling. I leaned against him, breathing his scent deeply into my nostrils. "They probably wouldn't look human either. They wouldn't need as much to eat or drink, as much sleep ..."

"As much oxygen," I mused. "Or maybe none at all."

"Engineered workers," he said. "Engineered lovers. Killers. Can't you just see the rich people? Living like gods on Mount Olympus. Living forever, using their toys up and just throwing them away. No guilt, because how can you feel sorry for something that doesn't feel sorry for itself?"

"How do you know what they would feel?" I asked. "The engineered people, I mean. John had feelings. I have feelings."

"You were supposed to. Workers wouldn't need to."

"They would have to think. Creatures that think can feel too."

He sighed. I could feel his chest expand and contract. "What's going to happen to the regular people?" he wondered. "You think they'll kill everyone?"

"That seems pretty outrageous," I said, but I thought about Mother and her remarks about diseases. "Maybe they would be too lazy to do it."

"Maybe not."

"Maybe they would be afraid."

"Afraid of what?"

I wasn't sure myself. I had to think about it for a long moment. "Being alone," I said at last. "Accidentally wiping the entire race out. I don't know."

Now it was his turn to think. "One thing that could happen," he said. "People could live longer and longer, have as many kids as they wanted, and the System would get really full."

"You think so?"

"Last year we were talking about a mission to Alpha Centauri."

"Really?" That made my ears perk up. I had never heard a thing about such a mission in the news net. All they ever did was talk about the fact that no one was doing it, that it was too hard, too expensive, too implausible. The idea was exciting. Rico thought so too, I could hear it in his voice.

"I sure would like to go on that mission," he said wistfully. I caught some of his excitement for a moment, but then the idea hit home.

"It would take so many years," I said.

"Yeah."

"I couldn't stand it if you went away that long, Rico."

His arms moved cautiously around me, and he pulled my face close to his. "Lucy," he whispered, "do you love me?"

"Yes."

"Do you love me because I'm like Joe?"

"I love you because you're like him, but also because you're not like him."

His lips pressed against my ear, and he unzipped my flight suit. His hand slipped inside and touched my breasts. I snuggled closer, trying to give him the best access I could.

"Where is he now?" he asked.

"I don't know. He may be dead."

"I hope he is." He kissed me before I could say anything about that, and his hands were demanding. He pulled my zipper all the way down and tore at my suit. I cooperated. My suit came off, and his followed. We pulled our bodies close together, kissing and holding, touching each other tenderly.

"Rico," I said, when he would let me talk again. "If Joe is dead, I'll need you more than ever."

"What if he's not dead? What if he's waiting for you?"

The idea hadn't occurred to me. But I talked fast, before he could assume the worst. "Listen, you and I are together for the duration, Rico. Don't you understand? Our enemies are too big to face alone. Ann and Joe are with us too, we'll need them like they need us. I won't give him up and I won't give you up."

"Maybe I'll just leave," he said, but he didn't sound like he meant it.

"Please don't leave."

"You'd better keep begging, Lucy. I mean it. If you want me to stay, keep begging me."

So I did. I begged him to stay, and soon I was begging him to do other things too. It made both of us feel a lot better.

◀◀ We're under the Tharsis dome," Rico said, waking me from my doze. Already I could feel the temperature rising. The wind had died down as the day progressed, turning gusty instead of raging. I had been able to see the volcanic terrain, and the farms, factories, and houses from a distance. But we didn't see one living soul the whole time.

"Are we almost where we're going?" I asked Rico.

"We'll be there about oh-three hundred hours," he told me.

"Where?"

"My house."

He didn't sound very happy about it. I couldn't blame him. We had passed through a ghost town early in the morning, and this had brought bitter memories back to Rico.

"The atmosphere bleeds off continuously," he had told me. "Did you know that?"

"Why?"

"Not enough gravity to keep it. That's why we finally needed the atmosphere plants. When I was a kid, I used to imagine that it would all bleed away in the night. I would lie in my bed and think it was getting harder and harder to breathe. This far north, the sky looks so strange. In the winter, you can't believe anyone could live here, grow things here. But they keep doing it."

We watched tumbleweeds blow across the empty road ahead of us, tangling in broken fences.

"New Barsoom is so different," I said.

"That's the best place on the planet. The warmest place. That's where they have the most money to feed into their dome, keep the temperature nice and summery."

"What season is it now, Rico?"

"Fall."

The sky did look kind of strange. The nights might have been longer too, I wasn't sure. I wasn't sure how long I was sleeping in between times.

"I'll bet you were happy to get assigned to New Barsoom."

"Everyone is. You hear about the rule?"

"The rule?"

"Good looks rule. Only the military is exempt. That's the only reason Chavez got in. He was an ugly cuss."

His voice had broken when he had said Chavez's name, and I hadn't known what to say to comfort him. Eventually I had fallen asleep, and we had passed under the dome.

I craned my neck to see if I could see a difference in the sky. Back in Arizona, the dome turned the sky sort of turquoise. I never knew if they did that because they thought it was pretty, or if it couldn't be helped. On special nights, they had programmed the star field on the dome to do interesting things, turn into dragons and whatnot.

The Tharsis sky was like sherbet.

"It's beautiful," I told Rico.

"Yeah."

"It feels a lot warmer."

"It gets up to about thirty degrees Fahrenheit in the winter," he said. "Sixty in the summer."

"That's not bad."

"Except at night. At night it gets cold enough to kill you. Lots of people die when they can't get back to shelter quick enough."

Back in New Barsoom, seventy-five-degree breezes had wafted through my open terrace door at night.

"I'll bet these weather domes stir up the dust storms," I said.

"They do, but no one wants to give up the domes."

"I don't blame them."

I glanced over at him. He hadn't been able to get as much rest as I had. He looked so tired. "Want me to drive for a while?" I asked.

He laughed.

"Seriously. Just give me directions, and you can sit on this side and nap."

"No, Lucy."

"Why not?"

He didn't answer.

"You think I'm a lousy driver? All I have to do is follow this road, right?" We had been on an old road since the day before. The terrain didn't look all that challenging at the moment.

His face could have belonged to a statue. But when I watched long enough I could see the muscle in his jaw jump. "What do you think I'm going to do, Rico?" I asked.

"Stab me in the back."

"What?"

"Why not, Lucy? Why should I believe anything you tell me?"

"You believed my body last night—"

"So? You were made for that, remember? I'll bet you even believe it when you're saying it. But I don't trust you too far, baby. I love you, but I can't help it."

He really meant it. I couldn't think of a damned thing that would change his mind. So finally I just said, "Okay, Rico. Do what you have to. Just tell me how I can help."

"I will," he said lightly. His tone of voice made me so mad, I almost slapped him. But I took some deep breaths and made myself look out my window until I wasn't mad anymore.

That took about two hours. Afterward I fell asleep again, this time for many hours. When I woke up, it was night, very cold, and we had crept into another town.

At first I thought it was a ghost town, but then I saw a few lights here and there. The place looked run-down, a lot like Glendale, which gave me an odd pang of nostalgia. Once we passed so close to a window we saw four people sitting at a table inside, and the six of us exchanged long looks while we rolled on by. There were three men and one woman, all looking their age, all drinking what looked like whiskey and smoking black cigarettes.

"You know them?" I asked Rico.

"I'm not sure," he said. "I haven't had much time for old neighbors in the past six years."

He didn't seem concerned about them, so I saw no reason to be nervous either. I thought about their faces, though. I had seen plenty of faces like that in Glendale. People who could afford nice hair, maybe get themselves a facial peel or a breast lift from time to time, but nothing fancy. I used to wonder how they could stand living that way.

"Why do you keep a house here when you don't live here anymore?" I asked.

"It's my mother's house. Where I grew up."

Would his mother be there? What would she think of me? Would she be in danger now that Rico was? Worry started to flutter around my head like an obnoxious moth, but Rico didn't look like he was in the mood for questions. I just sat there and kept it to myself.

About an hour later we pulled into the unpaved drive at the side of a dark house. There was a huge building out back, almost a barn, and both it and the house looked run-down and uninhabited. There were no lights on anywhere. Rico parked next to the back door of the house and turned off the engine. He stared at the house without saying a word.

"Is she in there?" I ventured. "Is she asleep?"

"She's dead."

"Oh."

"She walked out into the night ten years ago. We found her in the morning, freeze-dried, just sitting on a big rock like she was waiting for somebody."

"You lived here by yourself after that?" He would have been fifteen at the time.

"Yeah. Let me show you something."

I had thought he would take me into the house and reminisce about things in there, but instead we went to the big building out back. Rico grabbed a vertical bar and shoved hard, putting his entire body behind the effort. The wall moved two feet to the left, creaking painfully all the way. Rico disappeared through the gap and some lights throbbed on.

"Come in," he told me. I followed him, blinking as my eyes tried to focus on the object inside.

It was a stealth fighter, matte black in the shadows, but some indefinable color where the light struck its surface. The effect was to make it appear that chunks of it were missing. I had to get very close to find the Earth space-air markings on its side. I couldn't even tell how big it was except by comparing what I could see of it to Rico's figure crawling up its side.

"It was my father's," said Rico.

I stared at him until the different pieces began to come together in my muddled brain and form a picture. "Twenty-five years ago," I said. "You must have been born in the middle of the Mars Revolt."

"Yeah."

"And your father crashed here?"

"I've been fixing this ship since I was eight. My mother helped me with the money for parts. I was a pretty good mechanic, but I didn't finish it until just before I left for the academy."

"That's something," I said, very impressed with Rico and his ingenuity, and more than a little aroused.

"I guess I wanted to fly it back to Earth and find my father," he said, oblivious to my reaction. "I almost tried when I was fourteen, but I couldn't get the engines to fire."

I was wondering what branch of the service Joe had been in. I had always gotten the impression he was a marine, part of the shock troops that had been landed in the first week of the Mars Revolt, when they had thought it would be over in six weeks. Lots of those guys had been stranded with no support for two years, and I had always thought Joe was one of them.

But now here was Joe's mirror image standing next to me, talking about his Earth father. Maybe Rico's father was one of Joe's brothers, or cousins, or even Joe's father. Why not? I had an eleven-year-old mother myself, one who had grown me in a tank instead of her womb.

"Are you going to fly us out in this thing?" I asked him.

"It flies," he assured me. "I tested it just last year. I need to make some adjustments and transfer some power from the transport to the ship. It'll take a couple of hours."

He wasn't looking at me. He was climbing all over his ship, running familiar hands over its lines.

"Mind if I look at your house?" I asked.

"Go ahead."

I walked out and made for the back door, but then realized I didn't have a key code. I thought about going back to ask him for it. Instead I went to the back door and gave the knob a twist. It opened easily.

That gave me a twinge of paranoia. Were assassins waiting inside to kill us? But I doubted they would have waited. They would have just come out and dispatched us. I went in, my feet leaving footprints in the thick Martian dust on the floor.

The house wasn't a bad place. I had pictured poverty, but it actually looked quite livable. Maybe not modern and fancy like I was used to, but I could see that all of the necessities were there. What I couldn't see were signs of Rico's life. There were no pictures anywhere, none of an eight-year-old Rico working on his ship, or his pretty Hispanic mother, or of Joe sitting at the breakfast table with a cast on his arm.

There were two bedrooms. I had a hard time deciding which might have been Rico's, because they were both the same size and had identical beds in them. I pictured Rico lying on one of them, sucking in as much atmosphere as he could before it all bled away.

I found a bathroom. The water still ran in the sink, and the toilet flushed. Watching the water go down, I suddenly realized I had to urinate. It was nice to be able to undo my flight suit so easily and just sit down on the john in that nice big room instead of struggling in the cramped little portable in the transport. I sighed with relief. Whatever happened next, at least I wouldn't have to use that tiny john again.

I pulled my suit back on and wandered out to Rico's barn. He was working away. I sat down and watched him for a while, scratching absently at my right thigh. I had an itch there that just wouldn't go away.

Something moved under my suit.

I scratched again, and felt a small lump. "What the hell?" I asked aloud, scratching at it some more. Did I have some kind of swelling? How the hell did I get it? I started to unzip my suit, and I felt something tickle my back. I scratched just below my shoulder blade and found another lump.

I tore my suit off and looked at my thigh. A white beetle was attached to my skin there. I brushed at it, but it was stuck fast. I began to pull at it and realized that its head was completely submerged in my skin, along with all six of its feet, and something else too. A sharp appendage at the tip of its abdomen was pulsing in and out of my flesh, and I couldn't tear the damned thing off for the life of me.

"Rico!" I screamed.

He was at my side in seconds, but it seemed like forever before he was pulling at the beetle with a pair of pliers. That did the trick—at least party. He tore most of its body away, leaving the submerged parts while he turned me around and pulled four more of them off my back. I was crying hysterically by then, shaking with horror, but I stood submissively and let him do what he had to do while he searched my skin and pulled with the pliers.

Finally he picked me up and ran to the transport vehicle with me. He popped the hatch and pushed me in, pulling it shut after us, and immediately began to dig in the lockers, his movements urgent. A moment later he pulled out a big hypo and pushed it against my rump. I felt a sharp bite.

"What is that?" I asked him.

"The antidote," he snapped. "We have to get it in your system as fast as possible, before the parasites can take hold."

"The *what*?"

"Christ, Lucy, didn't you tell me you had the Blue Clap once? Don't you remember anything about that?"

I started to pant, but I couldn't catch my breath.

He had a small scalpel out of the medkit and he was cutting my skin where the bugs had dug in. After each incision he dumped a bunch of stinging stuff into the wounds and dabbed like mad.

"They laid eggs in me, didn't they!" I accused. He shook his head.

"Even if they did, the antidote will kill them. It's

been less than an hour, Lucy; you only have to worry if it's been one or two days."

"Then how come you're working so fast!?"

"I want to make sure! Don't you want me to make sure?"

"Yes!"

He cut and dabbed while I cried. My stomach was beginning to knot up, and my head pounded. But I started to calm down. He was right, he was doing the only thing he could do. I put my hand on his thigh and gripped the hard muscles there, taking as much comfort as I could from the contact.

"Now I remember," I told him. "They crawl on people when they're asleep. They have a natural anesthetic, right?"

"They're supposed to."

"When they're done, they crawl away, and you don't even know they've been on you . . ."

"That's when it gets dangerous," he said. "When people don't know and the parasites have a chance to invade your whole system, and then men pass them on to women in their sperm—"

"That's what happened to me. I mean, it *didn't* happen to me."

"Nothing's going to happen to you, Lucy. They probably didn't even lay eggs in you."

But he dabbed furiously, just in case.

"The house hasn't been sprayed since last year," he was saying. "But I don't understand how they got under your clothing."

"I went to the bathroom," I said meekly.

"Goddam, I should have warned you. I forgot all about it."

I began to fall asleep. I supposed the antidote was asserting its powerful forces over my body.

"I'm so glad you're here with me, Rico," I said, meaning it more than I had ever meant anything in my life. I felt his hard muscles under my hand and the stab of his scalpel in my wounds. I had never felt so safe in my life.

Rico woke me a little later, and the first thing I did was throw up. I felt so nauseated I could hardly stand it, and my head throbbed.

"I'm sorry, baby." Rico was pulling me into a sitting position. "You've got to have another shot, and then we have to go."

"Another shot?" I moaned.

"It won't be as bad as the first one. Your body gets used to it." He was already sticking it against my arm, so I just sat quietly while it stung me.

"We're going?" I asked, hoping I wouldn't throw up again.

"Can you walk?"

"You have to help me."

We staggered out of the vehicle. The ship was sitting at the end of the drive, giving off steam and making a humming noise. Vaguely it crossed my mind that it should have been exciting and interesting to fly in a stealth fighter. But I could only wonder if the g-forces of takeoff would make me throw up again.

Rico hauled me up to the rear cockpit and helped me get in. He fastened my straps, checked some equipment, then finally turned my face up and studied it. "You really feel lousy, don't you," he said.

"Yes."

He kissed my forehead. "I love you, Lucy."

"I love you too."

He smiled sadly. "You're turning green."

"It's okay."

"We could get shot right out of the sky before we even leave atmosphere. But if we engage it'll probably be in low orbit."

"What do you want me to do?"

"Just sit tight, sweetheart. Unless you're a gunner and I don't know it."

"I wish I were. Will you teach me someday, Rico?"

"That's a promise," he said, and he sealed my breathing mask over my face. He climbed down into his own seat, and the hatch sealed over our heads, making my ears pop.

Rico taxied the ship into the roadway, and then we sat there for what seemed like an awfully long time. I tried to look and see what was up head, but I couldn't see past him. I didn't know what to make of any of the screens in front of me, though they were all displaying information in pretty colors. Then, just when I least expected it, the engines fired, and we leapt forward and up at an incredible rate.

A giant hand squashed me back into my seat. I was thinking that at least when I was being pushed so hard I wouldn't be able to throw up. I could hardly even breathe. But then the forces let go, and so did I. I just had the time to pull my mask off first.

"I'm sorry, Rico," I said, trying to wipe stuff off monitors with my hands.

"You throw up again, baby?" he asked over my headphones.

"All over your equipment—"

"Don't worry about it, it's locked down."

I couldn't tell where the hell we were. We seemed to be traveling through a bluish-black limbo. But then a purple-red ball swung up underneath us. It was beautiful. I was looking out my side windows like a tourist, thinking, *This isn't so bad! If I weren't so sick, this could almost be fun.*

Another fighter pulled right up alongside us, smoother than a car on a roadway. I could see the guy who was sitting in the rear cockpit, looking back at me. I looked out the other window and found a fighter on that side, too.

Voices talked to Rico over our headsets, but it was military language, of which I could maybe understand every fourth word. "Is that you, Rivera?" Rico answered back plainly.

A man spoke to him again, and this time I was able to make out "—return to Tharsis Base immediately—"

"No," said Rico. His voice was calm, giving me the impression that he wasn't even alarmed. But then he said, "I won't let them kill me like they killed Chavez," with an intensity that brought tears to my eyes. He pulled away from them, and in another moment, something exploded in a silent, white flash on my left side.

"Are they shooting at us?" I asked stupidly.

I waited tensely for another explosion. None came. I heard voices over my headset, but they seemed to be talking to each other, not us. My stomach tensed up tighter with every moment that passed, yet the rest of my body was losing its strength. Before long I couldn't tell if only a few minutes or several had passed. I couldn't see the fighters anymore, but I could hear their voices over my headphones. I drifted into a doze and didn't know I had done so, because I was dreaming of the fighters. Every time I thought they had fired, I would wake to find that the status was unchanged.

When I had awakened this way for perhaps the hundredth time, I was startled by a green and blue luminescence spinning to the left and beneath us. But it was no explosion. It was the orbital colony, looming gigantically as we zoomed toward a landing strip at a horrifying rate. My body strained forward against the straps as we braked, and we slowed down to a much less frightening speed.

It was unreal. There was no sound when we touched and caught onto some sort of hook that we dragged along until it slowed us down and brought us to a halt. I couldn't hear the tow that tugged us into a hangar. Huge doors sealed behind us, and steam began to pour from thousands of spigots. After about fifteen minutes, I could hear their hissing. In another fifteen, Rico popped our hatch.

Rico was climbing down the side of the craft without helping me first, his face tense. I dragged myself up and peeked over the side, to find him standing rigidly and staring at something behind us. I looked, and saw two other fighter craft in the landing bay. They must have come in at the same time we did. Four men were crawling out and walking toward Rico, their hands hanging neutrally at their sides.

The man who reached Rico first had black eyes and auburn hair. A patch on his breast said "Rivera."

"Marte para Marcianos," said Rivera. Mars for Martians.

Rico let out a long breath and relaxed. He and Rivera stared into each other's eyes for another moment, in silent comradeship. Then Rico turned his eyes to me. He climbed up and gently helped me down from the craft. I could feel the men watching us.

The others had patches that said "Garcia," "Cervantes," and "Ernst." Ernst had white hair and blue eyes, but when he spoke it was with the same accent as the others.

"You must be Lucy," he said.

"Thank you for not shooting us down," I told them. Rico put an arm around me.

Before anyone could say another word, the huge compression doors on the station side of the bay hissed open, and ten guards marched through. Their weapons weren't drawn, and they didn't even look at us as they marched over to us. They stopped about four feet away from us and stood at attention. Rico and his friends positioned themselves so that I was behind them.

And then Red Hulot walked in. He marched quickly to where we were standing, passing the soldiers without the slightest concern. He halted about a foot from us, giving the other fighter pilots a glance, and then giving Rico a good, long stare. He seemed bemused.

"Son," he said, "you've got some mighty faithful comrades, that's a fact."

"I was counting on it," said Rico.

Red smiled and slapped him on the shoulder. "Come on in and let's talk about it," he said.

So in we went, Red's men marching in time behind us.

B y the time we had walked down several long halls
to a luxurious transport, I was ready to throw up
again, but I held on for dear life. Rico and Rivera
had to hold me up most of the way.

"Are you going to make it, Lucy?" Red asked with
concern as we sat down with six of the guards flank-
ing us and the heavy doors sealed behind us.
"Should I get you a doctor?"

"She was contaminated by leech beetles before we
left," said Rico, and Red's face became grim.

"That's a shame. I went through treatment for that
myself, back when I was doing survey in Tharsis."

I nodded, then regretted the movement. Finally I
just rested my head on Rico's shoulder, though I
tried to keep my eyes open and watch Red. I still
wasn't sure if we were safe or not.

"I'm sorry to say I didn't get your message until
an hour ago, son," Red was telling Rico. "Some buddies of mine in the service tell me someone was
murdered."

"His name was Chavez. I want to get these disks
to System News as fast as possible. They'll release it
to everyone."

"Paul and Charlotte Moisen are the people you
need to talk to. They're meeting us at my condo."

"Why are you here?" I asked Red. "I thought you hated the colony."

He laughed. "Just because you hate something doesn't mean you can't love it too. It's a long story."

"Not as long as ours, I bet."

"Maybe not." He looked at Rico again. "But I know two of those space-air admirals who are tied up with Designer Gene Co. I knew them when they were a couple of assholes at the academy. They haven't changed one bit."

Rico said something back, but my half-sleeping mind turned his words into nonsense. I felt someone dabbing at my face and hands with a wet-wipe, and I was given something fizzy to drink. Then we were getting out of the transport, and Red was talking into a wristphone.

"Keep them in receiving, dear," he ordered somebody. "Tell them we're having technical difficulties. And send that other squadron up from C section."

"Who?" I asked. "Who's coming?"

"Admiral Coltrane, for one," said Red. "He brought some boys with him, but not all of them are obeying his orders." He winked at Rico. "You Mars boys are an independent lot."

"How many court-martial orders has he filed so far?" Rico asked lightly.

"Two hundred three at our last count, but they'll never go through. I've already filed charges against *him*. I sure hope you've got something to show me that'll back me up."

We were being marched into his condo by then, a heavily fortified section of the station that looked like it could break away and maintain itself independently if necessary. I wondered if it had its own engines. We went through some pressure doors, surrounded by men talking on wristphones and men with shock armor and some strange-looking guns. Red kept up a constant stream of orders on his own phone. When he paused for a moment, I asked, "Is this station under attack?"

"Yes and no," he said. "We'll know for sure within the next six hours or so."

We were ushered from a security lock into a luxurious reception room. There were at least two dozen men and women sitting on couches and chairs around a big screen, waiting for us. They were all youngish, but none of them appeared to be using Rashad's color viruses. Some of them, like Paul and Charlotte Moisen from System News, wore press badges, but others had such an air of importance about them that they didn't seem to need identification.

"All right, folks," ordered Red. "Let's get this show on the road."

Rico handed him the black case, and we all sat down.

"Designer Gene Co., along with admirals Coltrane, Marquez, Norton, and Shaw of the Martian space-air force and generals Burgess and Tellez of the marine corps are plotting to murder top scientists and executives in Biotech Unlimited and YoungTech," began Rico, jumping right into his narration with a communiqué from General Burgess discussing "necessary elimination" of someone named Carol Greely. I heard a gasp from the end of my couch and saw a dark-skinned woman with features like Queen Nefertiti turn sort of a pale gray. I thought it was a pretty good guess that her initials were C.G.

"These *eliminations* have been ordered to prevent the development of bio-engineered life forms that might conceivably compete with the development of Operation Shock Troop, a plan to revolutionize the concept of warfare and facilitate the domination of the solar system by a secret Mars Consortium, under the direction of System president Andrew Pidgeon."

This statement provoked incredulous laughter until Rico backed it up with some video of what looked like an elite core of Special Forces marines on a hillside somewhere in the Tharsis region. They appeared to be on the alert for trouble and were moving cautiously through a light dust storm, when suddenly part of the hillside seemed to break away from itself and attack them. They were all dead within moments. Rico ran the killing scenes backward in slow-mo, and we saw the shock troops. They had six limbs and skin that changed color to match the surrounding terrain. When the marines were dead, they ate them, and disappeared back into their surroundings.

So no one laughed again. But a man with a name tag that read, "JOHN ANDERSON, CHANNEL 66 NEWS," asked, "What proof do you have that President Pidgeon is mixed up with this plot?"

Rico didn't bother to explain. Instead he showed another video. This one featured President Pidgeon and two anonymous men in blue suits. Pidgeon was saying, "I want to make sure that none of these murders can be traced back to me, understand? I'm not running this show, I'm just a spectator; because you and I both know, Jack—that we can't let Calvin and his lackeys get the presidency next election. There's just no way. We're in the toilet when that happens—so, you know—I'm not in the murder business, okay? I'm not giving the order to murder anybody. Understand?"

"Yes, sir," said an anonymous male voice.

"Good, because—this has got to be—one hundred percent—covered."

"Right."

"Just so we understand each other."

I could tell that this video had been filmed from someone's jacket button, but the image of Pidgeon was pretty crisp, and his mannerisms were well known to everybody. It was a very convincing video, and I'm sure Pidgeon already knew of its existence.

"That idiot," said Red. "He's just the sort of guy who would get himself blackmailed by amateurs."

"Bet you wouldn't make that mistake, Mr. Hulot," remarked a man with a badge that read "MARTIAN DAILY NEWS," and Red laughed.

"You're damned right I wouldn't, sonny."

We looked at a dozen more files and communiqués, demonstrating Chavez's obsessive pursuit of the truth. But the most convincing and horrifying pieces of evidence were those demonstration videos.

"Two other shock troop prototypes have been grown," said Rico, "each with different physical characteristics."

We watched them being put through their paces as they demonstrated their physical and mental superiority. We watched them kill *volunteers*, men and women who were obviously well-trained soldiers. And at last, we watched as they were destroyed, in an effort to demonstrate how difficult they were to kill. They were extremely difficult.

After four hours of it, Red switched on the lights. "I've got to file my evidence right now if I want to get anywhere with my charges," he told us. "I've got some high-speed copiers ready—you folks can start your broadcasts."

People who had been taking copious notes during Rico's narration jumped to their feet and hustled. Rico and his pilot buddies ran off with Red in one direction while everyone else scattered in every other. Only one other individual stayed seated with me. She was a breathtaking redhead who, along with Red, apparently felt that thirty-ish was the optimum age to be. She was studying me closely.

"So," she said. "You came out of a generation tank? You look too perfect to be an ordinary human being."

"How did you know that?" My nausea had died down, but I still felt like I wanted to go somewhere and sleep ten hours. I could barely muster any panic over her accusation.

"I'm an investigative reporter. Sarah Hulot." She extended her hand and I shook it weakly. By the time she had her hand back, I had made the connection.

"Hulot?" I asked. "Are you married to Red?"

"Thirty-five years this Tuesday," she said. "He pursued me so hard, I finally had to catch him. It's been a stormy relationship, but that's what keeps it fresh."

She was talking too much and too fast. She crossed her legs and lit a black cigarette with a hand that shook ever so slightly. Thankfully, the smoke blew in the opposite direction from where I was sitting. "I was Chavez's connection in the orbital colony," she said, looking at the floor as she said it. She took a deep drag and let it out slowly.

"His connection?"

"He came to me first, actually, over a month ago. He was beginning to find out some of the stuff we saw here tonight. I jumped on the opportunity to do a story like this. It was the biggest thing—I ever—" she took another long drag and blew it out so hard it seemed to shoot all the way across the room. "I urged him to find out as much as he could. God, he was a reporter's dream. Right inside, right on top of the goods. He didn't start to get scared until almost near the end. I started to get scared myself, to tell you the truth. I told him he should get out of there. I talked to him just an hour before he was killed."

Her voice cracked when she said, "He was killed"; I could hardly make out the words.

She couldn't seem to say anything more, though I could tell she wanted to. So we sat there in silence while everyone else made history.

I fell asleep on the couch. When I was asleep, I could still hear everyone talking excitedly. I would struggle awake, certain that something important needed to be attended to, that someone was speaking to me. But when I would wake, there would be nothing but silence.

You're alone, I would think, then fall helplessly back into sleep, where the cycle would start all over again. The voices, the struggle, consciousness and revelation, weakness and a long, long fall. It seemed to go on forever. I could get no rest, but I could never really achieve wakefulness.

At one point I heard Rico say, "It's the antidote working its way through her system. That cure is almost as bad as the disease."

"Help me!" I tried to call. I thought my mouth was moving, and I hoped I was making a loud enough sound to alert him, but he wasn't even there to begin with.

"You know what worries me?" I dreamed Red telling a mysterious someone who stood just out of sight. "What if they didn't kill all of those damned shock prototypes? What if they sent a couple of them up here? What the hell are we gonna do about it?"

I struggled awake to find darkness, silence, no Red and no one else either. "Help me," I called, and fell asleep again.

"I hope you've enjoyed your new skin, dear," said the mysterious someone, stepping out of the shadows as I fell asleep again. "Because I'm going to tear it off you strip by strip. I think you should have scales, and then I'll sell you to Meyer Finklestein."

She leaned over me, her long hair trailing into my face. But when I looked for those lovely, hated features, I found a skull instead. The only thing I could recognize were her eyes, green jewels set in black sockets. "This is the new thing, Lysel," she told me. "The cutting edge. How do you like it?"

"Rico!" I called, and I heard the sound of running feet. Men were shouting information at each other, cutting each other off in their eagerness to report information. Then I thought I heard Red saying, "—power is cut station-wide except for Emergency Life. We've got to get troops down to—"

A warm hand touched my cheek, and Rico's voice said, "—safe here—"

"Wait!" I pleaded, and this time when I woke up I took several deep breaths, flooding my system with oxygen. Soon I was able to sit up, and after another moment I got my eyes all the way open for about five seconds. I had to close them again, but I pried them open as soon as I could. I was able to take a longer look around.

The place had been locked up tighter than a drum. Someone had pulled a throw over me, a soft iridescent thing, turquoise, green, and lavender. I ran my hand over its soothing textures and wondered where Rico was.

He and I had been alone together in close quarters for longer than I had ever been with another human being.

"Rico?" I called hopelessly. I got up and searched the walls for light switches, but the whole room must have been controlled by a hidden console. I looked out a large panoramic window, and there was Mars, moving with the rotation of the station, as if it were orbiting us instead of the other way around. It was a purple ball with spots of blue and red. Its beauty comforted me.

No ships were in sight. I had expected a raging space battle to erupt around the station at any moment. Not this silent, empty nothingness.

"What's going on?" I called, mostly out of frustration. My voice echoed back at me from the thick transparency.

What if they didn't destroy all those shock prototypes? Had Red really said that, or was it just my own brain trying to tell me something?

What if they sent a few of them up here?

The faces of the engineered shock troops swam

before my eyes, human in some odd and disturbing ways. For instance, they could look quite recognizably happy, especially when killing or eating.

There was an elegant wet bar against one wall, near the panoramic window. I went to it in search of something to drink, something carbonated, since my sore stomach was beginning to flutter again. But I forgot about that when I found the flashlight in the cupboard with the glasses, a huge thing that was as big as some of the larger metal penises you could buy for your Machine. It was heavy too, pulling the muscles in my forearm when I tried to hold it at waist level. I thumbed it on, and an intense white light flooded across the room in an expanding circle.

The front door opened easily into the lock when I tried the controls, but the outer door was a little harder. When I pressed the opening bar, a message flashed on the little screen just above it:

Emergency Systems Activated Open Door Manually

I couldn't imagine how to do that. I shone my light on the panel and searched until I found a little key that said HELP. When I pushed it, I had to key my request in with the miniature keyboard. I pushed RETURN, and the panel beeped. Then it said:

Consult Owner's Manual

"Thanks a lot." I was about to turn away when a diagram of the door popped onto the screen, with green lights showing me how to get to the manual opening mechanism. It was easy. I popped the door open and shoved it aside.

The hallway beyond was pitch black.

"Hello?" I called. No one answered. "Rico? Red? Anyone?"

No one. My light shone down a long emptiness, fading out before it could reach the end.

Where the hell was everyone? Were they dead? If they had gone to do something important and/or dangerous, why had they left me alone?

I considered going back into the reception room, but only as a gesture, a pretense of good sense before taking the plunge. Behind me, the door slid shut.

I jumped like a cat and turned to look at it. Those systems were supposed to be off, so how had it closed? Maybe the thing had a battery. Anyway, there was no point in standing there like a scared child, gaping at it, so I turned my back on it and started off.

The hall was a lot longer than I had remembered, and when I reached its end, I found another air lock to struggle through. The lock opened into a tran-way that looked several miles long. No transports were in sight, though some amber emergency lights shone at even intervals along the wall. I decided to turn right and walk along the pedestrian path.

My heels made a muted clap, clap, clap, as I walked along, evoking memories of the sound of hooves on a floor. When I had passed the seventh set of lights, the power suddenly flickered on, making the transport rail ten feet below me pop and crackle in an angry fashion. But five seconds later it was off again, leaving me in total darkness with my heart pounding.

I stood there a moment and caught my breath.

"Lyyysssseeeellllll," called a soft voice, echoing down the transport tunnel. I spun and shone my light behind me. No one was in sight, but I didn't doubt my senses.

"Mother?" I called.

She giggled.

I turned and ran as fast as I could in the opposite direction. My stomach rebelled and my muscles cramped, but I kept going, hugging my flashlight to my body as if it were some great prize I was trying to protect.

I ran for a good fifteen minutes before my calves froze up and I went crashing to the sidewalk. The pain was unbelievable. I had to forget all other considerations for at least a full minute and rub them until they unclenched.

"It's that nasty Blue Clap antidote, isn't it, dear?" said Mother. She was standing about ten feet away from me, her hair unbound and her girlish body clad in a filmy, multilayered dress that floated on a nonexistent breeze. She took three slow steps toward me, and her face appeared in the amber light. She gave me that lovely smile I so dreaded, but her eyes were no longer confident, not the least bit mischievous. They sparkled, yes, the madness finally revealed under the layers it had taken her three hundred years to accumulate.

I vomited. Nothing came up but water.

"You can't vomit them up, Lysel," she sighed. "They have to eat their way out."

"Shut up!" I spat. "I'm sick of your—"

Really, I couldn't put into words what she was to me. She came closer, lifted something in her right hand. It was a gun with a barrel shaped like a penis. She pointed it at me.

"Is that a—" I was going to say "force gun." Fear made my throat close around the words.

"Look," she said, and aimed the gun about a foot

from where I was sprawled. A thin stream of liquid hit the ground, and she giggled. A water gun. But then the pool evaporated, turning to smoke.

"Acid," said Mother. "It hurts. I tried it out on Devil to make sure."

"God damn it." Tears filled my eyes, and I began to sob. My right hand clenched around the flashlight. She couldn't see it from where she was standing.

"Your face is all twisted up," she said, creeping closer, the gun aimed at my chest. "What's the matter? Did you like him, Lysel? I'm so sorry. He was my property, you know. You had no business going near him."

"You know what, Mother?" I whispered, and she had to lean closer to hear me. "He told me he thought you were an ugly old hag."

She lifted the gun to my face. I lunged, seizing her wrist, and the stream of acid went past me, striking the sidewalk and spraying a few small droplets on my coveralls. I felt the tiny burns, but I ignored them as I swung the flashlight with all my might and connected with the side of Mother's head. I heard a small *crunch,* and she crumpled like a pile of laundry.

I let go of her limp wrist and vomited again.

"My God!" someone was shrieking. "My *God!*" Rashad was running toward us, a black form throbbing in the amber light. He swooped down on Mother, his face wet with tears, and cradled her head gently in his hands. "Ozma," he sobbed. "My Ozma . . ."

"She—" I gasped, "was going—to—"

"God damn you!" he screamed, yellow eyes burning with hatred and grief. "You filthy whore! After all I did for you! I was the one who begged her to spare you! I was the one who deprogrammed your repulsion command! Me! And look what you do to repay me, you—you—!"

"Acid," I said. "Acid in the gun." But he was stroking her hair, pulling it away from the bloody spot on her head. "My beautiful Ozma. My sweet lover." He picked her up, careful to support her damaged head. Blood dropped to the sidewalk in fat little spatters. He stumbled off with her and disappeared.

In another moment the lights flickered on. The power rail crackled to life, and a transport came roaring down the track. I flattened myself to the ground as something exploded over my head, and then the transport was past me, zooming into the vanishing point so far down the line.

The wall behind me had a black burn with a big hole in the middle. Grief must have spoiled Rashad's aim. The relief was just beginning to sink in when I heard the transport coming back. I got up and ran, hoping to find a door before he could shoot at me again.

The transport slowed down as it pulled even with me, and the door popped open. I flattened myself against the wall and held the flashlight like a club.

Rico stuck his head out the door.

"Lucy, what the hell is wrong with you?"

"Nothing," I gasped, and threw up again.

I awoke in the middle of our sleep cycle, soaking wet. Mother had been chasing me down the tunnel in my dreams. Every time I woke from that dream, I was more certain she wasn't dead.

"Rico?" I whispered. My belly was pressed to his back, the two of us squeezed close together in our little cabin. He turned his head and said, "I'm awake."

"What are you thinking about?" I asked him.

"Shock troops."

"Red's men didn't find—"

"They're not supposed to be found. That's one of their selling points."

Mother and Rashad hadn't been found either. Hasagawa and six other doctors had been arrested, but released a day later. Of course there was no sign of the beautiful new "Machines" or of poor Devil. My John Carter.

"Are you sorry you didn't stay?" I asked him for the hundredth time.

"Yes," he said, this time.

I didn't chide him about it. I wasn't the one who told him to go. Red was. Not even Red could block the court-martial once it got started, despite the overwhelming evidence in Rico's favor. And despite the fact that the men who had filed the charges against him were now in prison. President Pidgeon was being called upon to resign; but there was still so much poison in the Mars Consortium, it probably wouldn't matter.

"They'll never straighten it out," Rico said.

"Then you're better off out of there."

"I'm running away."

Me too. From her. I wouldn't have long before Rashad fixed her head. I could picture him in a secret laboratory, bending over that little body.

I almost looked over my shoulder at the hard copy of L. Frank Baum's *The Land of Oz*, which was sitting on my night table next to my water and some mild sedatives. I had seen the title while I was perusing the ship's library bulletin, so I checked it out of the children's section. The illustrations by John R. Neill were delightful, but it was the story that held most of my attention.

Ozma was an eternally adolescent girl who ruled the Land of Oz, where no one ever grew old or died. Neill's illustration of her looked remarkably like Mother. But before Ozma became queen of Oz, she had been a boy, hidden from the eyes of her enemies by magic. I wondered if Mother had ever been a boy, or ever wanted to be. If anyone could have pulled off that sort of magic, she could.

"Lucy, you're shivering." Rico turned and pressed his belly into mine. He kissed my forehead, wrapped his arms around me and pulled me tight.

"Are you nervous about seeing Earth?" I asked him.

"No."

A world of feeling lurked behind that answer, but I couldn't sort it out. I wasn't nervous, either. I wasn't even scared. I wanted back into my own territory. I wasn't sure exactly what Rico and I would do once we got back to Phoenix, though I thought face sculpting would be a good start.

"How do you know Joe is still alive?" Rico whispered. He hadn't asked me that question since Mars. I still couldn't answer it.

"We'll see," I said. "One more month, and we'll be home."

If I had been looking out our little view window just then, I would have seen no movement at all, nothing to indicate how incredibly fast our ship was going. But I knew we were getting close to Earth. I could feel it. They were increasing our spin as we got closer, simulating gravity. We would be ready for Earth.

I drifted, safe, for the moment, in Rico's arms. Our chronometer ticked away the seconds on the wall across our tiny room; and as I fell asleep the *tick, tick, tick,* became the *CLUNK, CLUNK, CLUNK,* of hooves on a marble floor.

My new name was Lucinda Morano. Rico was Mr. Morano to my Mrs., picking the name Ernest to be his moniker. I called him Ernie.

"Good morning, Cinda," he said as we had breakfast together at Mi Patio restaurant, his first day on Earth.

"Good morning, Ernie," I said back.

"That should be 'Nesto.' "

"You want to be Nesto?"

He thought about it while he chewed on his breakfast burro. I could tell he already liked Phoenix food very much. "Naw," he said finally. "I like the way you say 'Ernie.' "

I closed my eyes and breathed in the Phoenix air. Every nuance of odor brought back feelings, memories of daily life. Stepping down off the passenger stage at Sky Harbor had been an incredible feeling, and the tears in my eyes hadn't been just from the bright Arizona sunlight.

After breakfast we took the subway to Glendale, to Joe's old store. My stomach fluttered all the way over there. I kept picturing Joe in his back room, polishing his guns. I pictured the look he would have on his face when he saw me, imagined myself kissing him, worried about how Rico would feel about the whole thing. But I needn't have worried.

Joe's shop had burned to the ground. No one had even bothered to build a new one in its place.

"You need to go have a drink?" Rico held my hand while I stood there and gaped, my mind empty. He had to ask me twice before I understood him.

"Yes."

So we went back to Phoenix and I had *two* drinks. "God damn her," I said several times while Rico squeezed my knee or my shoulder or any other body part that seemed handy, and said, "You got her good, baby. You got her back."

I supposed I had, whether she was dead or not. That brain injury would take a lot of RNA programming to function properly again. That was something.

"Let's look for a place to live," I said.

I hadn't really expected to find a place, not that same day, but the third house we looked at was the one. It had wooden floors and a wonderful bathroom full of green tile and porcelain. What I liked the most was that you could see everything around you from all directions but couldn't be seen back. Whoever had planted the shrubbery must have done that on purpose.

"We'll take it," Rico told the lady, and plunked down six months of the credit Red had loaned us.

The very next thing we did was plug into the news and communication nets. I put an ad for my business in the directory along with a picture of myself. By evening I had ten calls on the line.

The only other thing we did that day was buy a bed. We had it delivered that afternoon and immedi-

ately made it ours. Later, as Rico lay on top of me
and my business line rang off the hook in the other
room, he asked me, "You gonna support me, baby?"

"If you want," I answered, knowing perfectly well
that he was joking. No pilot could stop being a pilot.
Besides, we were going to need access to aircraft if
we were going to find Joe's old Fortress of Solitude.

I gazed at Rico's body and imagined that he was
Joe. His face was nuzzled into my neck, so I could
do it secretly. I kissed Joe's beautiful shoulders,
licked the lobe of his ear.

"Baby," murmured Rico.

I admired the blue shadows under Joe's close-cut
hairline, the classic angle of his jaw, the muscles of
his arms. I wrapped my legs around the backs of his
knees and pulled him closer.

"You want it again, Cinda?" whispered Rico. He
gave me a soft bite on the neck, and I felt his penis
hardening. I didn't answer, just kept kissing and
touching him, until we both knew the answer was
yes.

In the morning I played my messages from the day
before. I got my ten clients lined up, one by one,
then listened to the last two calls on the line.

The first was from Linda Tree. I didn't have my
vid receiver hooked up yet, but I recognized her
voice immediately.

"Jesus, Lucy, what the hell are you doing back on
Earth? Are you crazy? Any fool can find you with
your picture in the directory, for chrissake. Listen, I
need to talk to you as soon as possible. Call me. I'm
still at the old address. You wouldn't believe everything that's been going on! Just call me, okay?"

The second message was from Scorpianne.

"I'm working at Funny Stuff these days," her voice whispered over the line. "Come up and see my show some time."

I wrote the name "Funny Stuff" on my message pad and began to look for it in the directory.

I agonized about my decision not to tell Rico about Scorpianne's call, but it seemed the right thing to do. He would have wanted to go down there immediately and call her out. He was still too mad about what had happened on Mars to think clearly about what was happening on Earth. As it was, he needed that fire to go find a job.

He found kindred spirits down at the Phoenix Heliport and got hired the very same day.

"They've got a flying club," he told me with a wink. "We're in, baby."

But he wanted to come with me to see Linda, and I was relieved to have him. Because I had a premonition how she would still look these days. And I was right. She came to the door in a little girl's body. The sight made my stomach flutter.

"Who's he?" she asked me, before she even said hello, peering past me at Rico in the hall.

"This is my husband, Ernie Morano," I said.

"Oh." She still wouldn't open the door to her middle-class apartment. "That's why you're calling yourself Lucinda Morano, huh? I thought you were hiding or something."

"If I were trying to hide, why would I have put my picture in the directory?"

"Oh, right." She finally opened the door and let us in. I glanced around the room at her bland rental furniture, which was arranged without the slightest concern for aesthetics. Meanwhile, she was giving Rico the eye, trying to see if he was the sort to go for little girls.

"God, Lucy," she said finally, "you look—I can't believe it! Is Mars that far ahead of us in Youth Technology?"

"How did you know I was on Mars?"

She shrugged and looked away, then plopped herself down on the circular couch. Rico and I sat too.

"Jeez," she said, staring at me again. "You could be seventeen, Lucy. I mean it. You looked good before, but *this*—"

"I thought you were going to get changed back, Linda."

"Changed back?"

"To a woman's body."

"Can't afford to." She grimaced, and her face became twenty years older. I could tell she had had some fancy surgery, maybe some peels and even some skin regeneration. But she was no Ozma, that was for sure. "Six hundred thousand doesn't buy as much as it used to. I was lucky to get out of that fucking hospital intact."

Rico was leaning forward, his face neutral but intent. I used my acting ability and leaned back, relaxed and confident. If I had been a smoker I would have been dangling a cigarette. Instead I crossed my legs and dangled my foot.

"Have you made up with Machine Co.?" I asked, implying that *I* had.

"Sure, you kidding?" she snorted. "What else? They gave me a new Machine, free of charge. But I hardly get to use it anymore."

"Oh?"

"Jeez, Lucy, how long have you been away? There's a new thing these days."

"What is it?"

"It's the fuck-in-person thing, that's what. I had to send Tracy away to her grandparents' house. No way can I have her around with a bunch of strange men coming in. The other day I caught her doing a striptease for one guy—"

And she rambled on about it for another half hour. I made sympathetic noises without really paying much attention, but poor Rico sat there looking horrified. I patted his knee. Finally I broke in and said, "There's no market for video at all, anymore?"

"Yes, but it's been cut in half. I have bills, you know?"

"Yes," I agreed, privately assessing the strain in her face and adding the drug element into the equation. Probably there was a pimp in the picture too. Pimps always came with the in-person trade. Fucking parasites.

"But you know what?" she concluded. "I'm thinking of becoming a stripper."

I raised my eyebrows. Stripping in front of a live audience had been considered quite perverse when I had last been on Earth. But as Ozma had said, today's Perverse is tomorrow's New Thing.

"I've already got my act down," she was saying, and she launched into a description of a performance that included a tricycle and masturbation with a candy cane. She sneaked peeks at Rico as she talked, her eyes glittering.

"I've got an audition tomorrow night," she said.

"Would you mind coming along and sitting in the audience to give me some moral support?"

"Where?" I asked.

"Funny Stuff. It's in Tempe, but it's a good place to make money. People come to that joint from all over the valley."

Her eyes darted about the room, anywhere but at me. Christ, but Linda was stupid. Did she think Scorpianne would give her money for helping out? It made me a little sad. Back when we had all been video sisters together—me, Linda, Wendy, and so many others—we had felt affection for each other, even when we didn't really like each other.

"Can't tomorrow night," I told her. "Maybe next week?"

She frowned. "What's this about you doing face sculpting? When did you get into that?"

"On Mars."

Her eyes got wide. "You must make a lot of money these days."

"Enough."

Her eyes narrowed again. "More than a video prostitute, I bet. I wish I could do that sort of thing. How do you get into that field anyway?"

I looked at her apartment, so utterly devoid of beauty and charm. "Years of study," I said. "It's not easy, Linda."

Her face fell. "God, I hate the way things are turning around. Remember the video days, Lucy? You never had to let one of those SOB's touch you. You could turn them off any time you wanted. I used to do that sometimes. I would say, 'time's up!' at exactly five P.M. and cut some guy off right when he was about to come. I got such a kick out of that."

"You must have lost a few clients that way."

"So? It was part of my act, Lucy. I was a nasty little girl and I acted like one. Now I have to suck their cocks." She glanced at Rico again. "I'm not afraid to say that. I suck cock better than anyone you ever met."

Rico didn't answer.

"How's Wendy doing these days?" I asked her.

"Huh?"

"Wendy the hermaphrodite."

"Oh. Okay, I guess. I haven't talked to her in a few weeks."

Not surprising, since Wendy had been dead for a couple of years. "Well, I guess you've been busy. Frankly, I'm surprised you trusted Machine Co. enough to let them give you another Machine. That's why I got out of the biz."

"That's funny, Lucy," she snarled. "*Let* them? The fucking thing showed up on my doorstep one day, and I knew better than to make them think I didn't trust them anymore. You know what happens to people who know too much?"

"No. What?"

"Very funny. Look, did you say you could come to the club with me next week?"

"Sure."

"How about Wednesday? Seven o'clock?"

"Right."

"You can pick me up here. I'll bet you have your own private car these days."

"No, but I'll hire us a cab. My treat. For old time's sake." I smiled warmly, and she gave me a barracuda grin in return.

* * *

"If you don't mind, I'd like to stay home next Wednesday," Rico told me on the subway. "I like to watch women dance naked, but I've got a sleaze limit."

"You'd be amazed at the amount of squirt a good sleaze can squeeze out of you," I said.

"Really? You ever dance naked, Lucy?"

"For video clients."

"Will you do it for me?"

The idea sent a thrill up my spine. Just imagining it got me so excited I started to tremble. Rico moved closer and pressed his mouth to my ear.

"Tonight?" he asked.

"Yes."

"I'll be thinking about it all day."

"Me too."

But he had to be at work in an hour, so we disengaged and I tried to calm down again. It helped to think about Scorpianne and Machine Co.

"What are you going to do today?" Rico asked me.

"Talk to three clients and find a good surgeon to work with. But I want you to stay in touch, Rico. Call me at regular intervals, okay?"

"Right."

He got off at the Sky Harbor station, and I went on to Phoenix. But I got off five stops early and made a call from a public vidphone. I had a hunch.

"Machine Co., please," I told the operator.

She connected me with a lovely young woman. "To whom do you wish to speak?" she asked haughtily, causing me to raise my estimate of her age.

"Oh, I'm not sure," I said, looking embarrassed. "This is Linda Tree calling, and I just need to, you know, talk to someone who can help me—"

"One moment," she interrupted, and I was instantly connected to the executive who had handled my complaint two years before. When he recognized me, his face revealed astonishment for the barest moment, confirming my hunch.

"Don't hang up," I said quickly. "Just hear me out. We have some important things to talk about."

"Like what?" he said without inflection.

"Like Ozma."

"Go ahead."

"I've seen the new Machines," I told him, but his pale face was back to its lifeless mode.

"You're referring to the Machine X 7001," he said. "Are you interested in speaking to a salesperson?"

"I'm referring to the vat people."

Outside the booth, horns honked and people shouted. Inside, he and I were quiet.

"Well?" I said at last.

"I don't know what you want me to say, Ms. Cartier."

"Tell you what. I'll give you something if you give me something."

"Yes?"

"Do you know where Ozma is right now?"

"If that's what you wish to know, you're out of luck, Ms.—"

"No. In return for the story of what's happened to Ozma, tell me whether or not Machine Co. has separated from Designer Gene Co. I want to know if you're still part of their package."

"We're not," he said. "They had—conflicting goals."

"I know. All right then. Ozma was badly injured

on the Mars orbital colony. She had the left side of her skull caved in with a large flashlight."

He steepled his fingers, hiding his mouth behind the pyramid they created. "Your flashlight?" he inquired.

"Yes."

"Where is her body?"

"Rashad spirited it away."

"Was she dead?"

"I don't know."

He flexed his fingers up and down, but still managed to conceal the lower part of his face. "I had thought you and she were getting along rather well," he said.

"Are you kidding?"

"After all, you were her daughter."

"So?"

"Like mother, like daughter, then. You're not the typical female, Ms. Cartier." His dead eyes examined me without blinking. I wondered if they were mechanical implants.

"I don't know what you mean," I said.

"You're not sentimental, emotional. You're not weak. By the way, sorry about your male friend. Mr. Santos."

"Sorry?"

"The explosion. I'm told his body was not recognizable."

"I'm sure it wasn't."

He watched for my tears, which didn't come.

"Is there anything else you'd like from me?" he asked, as if he would really give something.

"No. You can forget about the settlement."

"Oh?"

"Mother's estate left me a large sum. I'm well taken care of."

He was silent. I smiled warmly, doing my best to emulate Ozma's particular expression.

"Thank you for your attention," I said, and severed the connection.

I waited until I was out of the booth and back on the subway before I let my face catch up with my feelings about Joe. I had mixed feelings actually, both hope and despair. After all, Joe was an expert at playing dead. He had done it before, so why couldn't he do it again?

At home, I looked up the local YoungTech hospital in the directory and sent them a query along with my résumé and photo. I got a call back within the half hour.

"Your face is impressive," said Doctor Khan, a beautiful woman with features to match her Arabic name. "Can we have lunch tomorrow?"

So I made a date with her, and then we chatted a little about Mars and how far Earth had to come to catch up. I cut things short with an apology. "I'm entertaining tonight," I said. "I have to pick up some things."

"I understand," she said. "Have a lovely party."

I stripped for Rico. I managed to draw the actual stripping out for a whole half hour, then danced naked for him, using every trick I had learned in thirty-eight years of video training. His face goaded me, inspired me to new heights, and when I couldn't stand it any longer, I finally kneeled in front of him and did what I had done in front of my mirror on Mars. His reaction was quite satisfying. He pinned me to the floor and played rapist, ravishing me with bites and kisses and soft little threats, then slowly fucked me into a wild, wonderful finale.

"I'd like to tie you up and spank you sometime," he said afterward, and before we knew it, we were off again. We didn't get to sleep until four in the morning.

My vidphone rang at four-thirty. I picked up the bedside audio, automatically. "Hello?" I mumbled.

"Baby, you're good," murmured a woman's voice.

"Huh?"

"You know what I'm doing now?"

"No. What are you doing?"

"I'm watching the video I made of you and your lover. My favorite part is the strip. I don't like to watch him fuck you, though. Maybe I'll cut his cock off."

"Scorpianne?" I whispered.

She hung up.

When Saturday rolled around, Rico and I met two of his new flying buddies at a nice little brewery-deli called Hops. Their eyes popped out of their heads when they saw me, causing a bit of a chill from their wives. But once the women found out what I did for a living, they warmed up considerably. I answered their questions while Joe talked the guys into flying over the desert for the afternoon outing.

Richard and Bob were retired space-air pilots, though outwardly they were as young as the new bucks, good-looking and sandy-haired. Perhaps they hadn't bothered to regenerate their inner organs— most men neglected to do that until something went terribly wrong. Except for their genitalia, of course.

I noticed Richard's wife, Sylvia, kept glancing down to see if I was having an effect on her husband's. Apparently I was; but instead of getting mad about it she asked me about my breast implants.

"Let's go to the ladies' room," I said, giving her a wink. She hopped up, grabbing Bob's wife, Toni, by the elbow, and the three of us continued our conversation in the smoking lounge.

"So what's it like having tits that big?" Toni asked me without malice. She had quite lovely small conical breasts, which she had taken the trouble to display in a spaghetti-strap knit, but she seemed fascinated by my breasts.

"You're not going to get implants, Toni," laughed Sylvia. "You know how much Bob likes those little-girl tits."

"Yeah, he likes legs and ass. But you've got those too, Lucinda. You couldn't have been born with those—?"

"No," I admitted.

"You don't strip, do you?" Sylvia half-whispered. She and Toni leaned forward, their eyes intent. "I mean, as a hobby."

"A hobby?"

"Sylvia's been doing it for two months now," giggled Toni. "She's got the tits for it."

"Not like yours," said Sylvia. "Honestly, are they heavy?"

I explained about the inner suspension, and as they listened I began to realize something. Neither of them was blinking. Their eyes seemed extraordinarily lustrous, too. Especially Sylvia's, which were a blue so light they were almost white, save for azure streaks running like spokes around the center and a pale gray outer circle.

"The bioimplants fuse with the glands," I said. "So there's no separation or dimpling, and there's no hardening of surrounding tissue. They feel real."

"God." Sylvia felt her own breasts absently. "I've gotten lifts, but never anything more. I'm a D-cup, you know? Usually people go down instead of up."

"You look good naked, Syl," said Toni. "You could make a living as a dancer."

"God, if Rich ever found out—!" Sylvia rolled her eyes, and they shared a nervous laugh. Meanwhile, I studied them. They were trim, their skin youthful and their hair thick and lustrous. They weren't quite up to the Mars level of youthfulness, but they were better than what I used to see on Earth.

"Do you know lots of women who strip for thrills?" I asked them.

"There are two places in town for amateurs," said Toni. "They're always packed. Men get excited to think they might get to see one of their friend's wives dance naked."

"What if they see their own wives?"

"Disaster," laughed Toni, but Sylvia just smiled softly. I had a feeling the idea pleased her.

After that they seemed to lose interest in the subject of implants and, in fact, in me. But once I got up, they hurried after me, as if fearful I would steal Bob and Richard.

"What the hell do you girls do in there?" Richard asked Sylvia when we got back, careful to keep his eyes on her instead of the new female in town. Sylvia just shrugged. Perversely, I answered him.

"We talk about things that would embarrass you," I said.

Rico squeezed my hand under the table.

The helicraft was very much like the one I had flown in over the central rift of the Valles Marineris, but this time Rico and I were up front so Rico could be copilot. Toni and Bob were in the observation bubble together. I was sitting between Richard and Rico, my eyes glued to a computer readout of the terrain. It was odd, but I found I could recognize things better that way.

"You folks seem to be looking for something," said Richard, a little too lightly for my tastes. He and Rico had already formed a closeness that astonished me, a bonding of kindred spirits. But I noticed there were some subjects they avoided completely. The Mars Revolt, for instance.

"I was here many years ago," I told him, not having to fake the emotion in my voice, "with someone I loved very much. Now he's dead, and I'm trying to find the place again."

"Hell, we can land if you want," said Richard. "If you find it, I mean."

"We should have brought a picnic," remarked Sylvia.

"No, I want to see it from the air," I said. "The view is so beautiful from up here."

"Not as nice as the Valles Marineris, I bet," said Richard. He didn't seem to mean anything by it, but Rico tensed. I put a hand on his thigh until he relaxed again.

"I think this is it," I said. The patterns on the screen were matching patterns in my memory. I looked out of the bubble, and there was the Fortress, Joe and Ann's secret mountain.

Rico looked to me for confirmation, then nodded briskly.

"Beautiful view," said Richard.

"Yes." I dabbed at the corners of my eyes, turning so he and Sylvia couldn't see my face.

Rico and I returned to the mountain after nightfall, in a rented jeep. I hadn't expected to find that things were still the same, so I wasn't surprised to discover that the door had been sealed up with concrete. Rico and I stood there in our black coveralls, looking like a couple of frustrated spies, until finally he turned to me and said, "They must still be alive."

"Huh?" That wasn't what I had been thinking at all.

"They moved their hideout. And no one built a new store over Joe's old one. Get it?"

"No."

"Because his buddies know he's not really gone. If they were dead, why would anyone bother to seal up this door? That's a lot of work."

"Maybe there were secrets here that Moth— Ozma didn't want revealed . . ."

"She'd just take them and go."

"What if she couldn't find them all? What if she needed to be sure?"

"She'd leave a sentry behind, she wouldn't seal the place up—" Rico stopped dead, listening. I listened too and heard the hum.

We turned and saw the Machine. It was a lot like the one Scorpianne had used to rape me at the Motel 62, except it had no penis. Beside it was a human

figure clad in black, just like we were, but with a
hood and mask to match. It was holding a control
box.

The Machine seized Rico and me like a spider seizing its prey. Neither of us bothered to scream. "Who
are you?" Rico asked the person in black. He/she
didn't answer, but walked silently beside the Machine as it carried us off into the night.

The Machine got into the loading bay of a small
carrier craft, taking us with it, and settled down to
the floor with us, still holding tight. The black-clad
person had walked around to the front of the craft
and was presumably getting ready to pilot it. But I
could feel him/her watching from the eyes of the
Machine, paying special attention to Rico.

A few moments later the Machine braced itself and
we felt the liftoff. The Machine was holding us just
firmly enough to keep us confined, reacting to movement by a momentary tightening of grip, but ad-
justing immediately once the movement stopped. I
decided to risk a question.

"Are you going to kill us?" I asked, putting an
edge of fear into my voice.

At first I thought I wouldn't get an answer, but
finally a woman's voice said, "No!" over the Machine's intercom. I thought I knew the voice then. I
gave Rico a reassuring look, but I could see the suspicion had already dawned on him as well.

About an hour later we landed again, and the Machine let us go. It folded itself into a corner and shut
itself off. Our door opened. The black-clad person
stuck her head in, but now she had her hood and
mask off.

"Ann," I said.

She gave me a weary smile. "Come on." She motioned for us to follow.

The new Fortress of Solitude was right next to Sky Harbor, which was pretty damned funny, though Rico and I weren't laughing. Actually it was the perfect hiding place, right out in the open. We walked into a car rental place, then took an elevator down into a complex that made Red's setup on the orbital colony look sloppy.

Ann finally paused in front of some armored doors. She gave Rico a long look, under which he seemed unnaturally still, then keyed some numbers into a panel. The door popped open, and we went into Ann's lab.

Joe was floating in a tank near the far wall. His hair had grown as long as mine in all that time, but Ann had tied it up, maybe so it wouldn't obscure his face.

Ann went to him and stood there with her back to us, her arms wrapped tightly around her body. She said nothing, and Rico seemed paralyzed, so I took the initiative. I approached her cautiously and said, "Tell me about the explosion."

She cleared her throat a couple of times. When she was ready, she said, "It was three months into your regeneration. Joe had some tracers out on Machine Co., and we both thought we had managed to keep the Designer Gene dogs from sniffing us out. After all, we'd been doing that successfully for years."

She turned her head to look at me, and I saw tears in the corners of her eyes. But she kept them in check. "Joe had volatiles in his shop, but he was careful to keep them separate. While he was out, someone mixed them together—so they would ignite when he flipped the light on. He was badly burned over one hundred percent of his body. In fact, he would have died within minutes if they hadn't had a portable tank ready for him."

She swallowed with difficulty. I felt Rico come up beside us, his eyes on Joe. Ann glanced at him, and the trouble in her eyes was momentarily replaced with wonder.

"They offered me a deal," she said. "Joe for you."

"Ah." Now I understood. I was frankly amazed that they had kept their end of the bargain. "He's been in there all this time?"

"The damage was more than skin deep."

"What about his brain?" Rico asked, and Ann jumped. His voice was very much like Joe's, only his inflection was different.

"No damage," she said, and indicated some connections that went from Joe's head to a nearby terminal. "I've been talking to his brain. He's confused, but sharp." She looked down. "He keeps asking about you, Lucy."

Her sorrow was so palpable I was overwhelmed by it. Several moments went by before I remembered to put my hand on her shoulder. The physical things were still hard for me, after all those years of phobia. But I think it made her feel better. Finally, she looked directly at Rico again.

"You're from the Tharsis region, yes?"

"Yes."

"Joe thought he might have a child on Mars."

Rico didn't answer that. His throat worked as if he were trying to swallow.

"He won't ask for your forgiveness," Ann warned him. "He's not like that."

"That's what my mother always said."

"I'm sorry." She kept looking straight at him, and finally he looked back. He seemed to like what he saw. Ann was very attractive, in a natural sort of way.

"You look exactly like him," she said.

"He looks younger."

"Not when he's awake. Not when he's—" she broke off, but I knew what she meant. Joe had an intensity that no young man could ever emulate. Even now, when he was unconscious, light seemed to shine from the narrow slits of his almost closed eyes.

I moved closer. I wasn't imagining the light. "Ann, are those eyes—"

"I knew he'd want to keep the engineered eyes," she said, turning back to the tank. "I could have grown him some natural ones, but he liked the special features."

"You can see farther," Rico said. "You can even hook into your shipboard computer and use them as a screen. Some pilots I knew had them . . ."

We had a long silence then, while each of us thought his or her own thoughts. But the longer I stood there, the harder it became for me to think clearly at all. I wanted to reach into the tank and stroke Joe's wet skin. I wanted to get Ann to let me talk to him on the computer. But Ann and Rico hindered me; I couldn't stop worrying about their feelings.

Rico was crying, silently and without a trace of

emotion on his face. Ann was close to tears herself. "Do you have living quarters in here?" I asked her.

She nodded. "Go to the end of the hall and ride the elevator down two floors. My room is the first on the left. You're free to use any of the others."

So I took Rico by the elbow and led him into a bedroom, where I made love to him. He wasn't feeling up to it, but I still managed to coax him into a climax. Afterward I lay beside him and stroked his hair until he fell asleep.

Then I went looking for Ann again. I found her in the hall. She looked as if she couldn't make up her mind about whether or not to knock on our door.

"I need to ask you a special favor," I said.

"I told him you're back."

"—Thank you—"

"You don't have to thank me, Lucy. I didn't want to give you up to her. But I love Joe more than my own life."

"Could you love Rico as well?"

She didn't blink. "That's an interesting question."

"For me, too. You're the only one I can trust to understand what I mean, Ann."

"I understand."

"Please take care of him for me. I need to get one more thing out of the way before we can all be together." I watched her to make sure she knew what I meant by *take care of him*. She did.

"Lucy, is Ozma still—"

"I bashed her in the head with a flashlight."

"I know." She glanced at Rico's door and lowered her voice. "I have connections on the orbital colony. Joe and I have been trying to follow your situation all along."

"Can I speak to him?"

"In an hour. He's in a rest cycle."

I sighed. "It'll have to wait. Scorpianne is expecting me Wednesday. I'm going to surprise her tonight."

"Lucy, don't. Why must *you* be the one—"

"I'm her sister."

She started to object, then changed her mind. She rubbed her face wearily, and I was intrigued to note that she still looked young in that condition. "If I had known who you were," she sighed.

"Would you have known?"

"I wasn't there when they were growing you. It wasn't my project. I would have had—objections."

She really didn't have to say those things. I was still more curious about something else. "How old are you, Ann?"

She cocked her head in a familiar, yet not familiar, fashion. "You have a right to know, I suppose. I'm over three hundred, Lucy. I have to work a lot harder than Ozma to stay young, to be twenty-one instead of eleven, but it's worth it. It's worth it to be a woman. You understand?"

"Yes."

"Good. Now come with me. I have a gun for you."

It was midnight when I got to Funny Stuff, but the place was jammed. I had to stand in back with a lot of men who seemed excited to see a woman spectator at a strip joint. A few other women were there too, but they were sitting at tables with dates.

Someone finally came around to take my order for a vodka tonic while an unspectacular woman postured about on the stage, rolling her torso and showing men her vulva. If she had been video, they would have changed the channel within a minute; but because she was live, they were enthralled.

"You a dancer?" a man pushed closer to ask me.

"No," I said.

He stared for a long moment, as if unsure how to interpret my answer.

"You a lezzy?" he asked at last.

"Not exactly." I lowered my voice several octaves. "I just got implants and electrolysis, but I'm not getting the complete sex change. I kind of like having a dick."

He moved away.

Linda had been right when she said people came there from all over the valley. Every economic class seemed to be represented. It turned my stomach a little bit. I still preferred the clean contact of video when it came to the sex industry. And I was a little annoyed with the strippers too; they weren't good actresses. They didn't look excited about what they were doing, and it detracted from their performances. Why was the place so crowded? By the end of my second drink I was bored and almost ready to call it a night.

Then Scorpianne came out.

The room had gotten very quiet after the last dancer left, and the people in back had surged forward, some of them trying to push me ahead of them until I rewarded them with a well-aimed elbow or two. I let them flow past me and moved into the shadows. From offstage I could hear a familiar sound:

CLUNK, CLUNK, CLUNK, CLUNK . . .

I waited, expecting to see red skin. But the creature who stalked out onto the stage had skin three times whiter than milk. Only her nipples had any color. They were blood red, and I don't think they were rouged.

She had her brother's beautiful face, and she had his height. She had the widow's peak, only with white hair flowing from it. But she wasn't like him at all. She wore an expression that made me press my back against the wall and put my hand on my hidden gun.

Someone turned on a recording of a flute, and Scorpianne began to dance.

This wasn't the tease and wiggle the other dancers had done. She pounded her strength and pride and anger into our skulls until I thought the stage would break. She mesmerized with cold eyes and sharp hooves, red nipples and a red vulva that was like a bleeding mouth. Her scent drifted over and into the audience, weaving it all together until it wasn't specifically male or female, but sex in its purest, rawest state. I began to long for Joe and Rico. After a while, I almost wished that sleazy guy would come back and proposition me again. I might have a different answer for him.

The music stopped and she left the stage. For a moment we all stood or sat there, panting and dazed. But after a moment she came back with a big black whip, her cruel face now twisted into the most chilling look of contempt I had ever seen.

The audience started to clap their hands rhythmically, and she moved her body in time with them, coiling and uncoiling the whip. A man threw a wadded-up bill at the stage. She struck like lightning with that whip, knocking him right out of his chair. Instantly more bills landed at her feet and she obliged by whipping the donors. But she didn't bend to pick up the bills, and after a while she was whipping people whether they threw money at her or not. Soon she had marked every man and woman within reach. I was glad to be out of her range.

It went on long enough for me to drink another vodka. I probably drank it too fast, but I needed it. For courage, among other things.

When Scorpianne left the stage she kicked bills out of her way like trash. A little man scurried in and scooped the money into a bucket. A lot of people left at that point; those who remained sat at the tables, calmly drinking, their eyes shining.

No one tried to stop me when I went backstage.

She was easy to find. Her dressing room door was

open. She sat in front of her mirror, still naked, turned slightly so she could see the reflection of anyone who came in. When she saw me, her eyes burned with triumph.

"I like your act," I told her.

She pointed to the chair next to hers. "Sit down."

A voice at the back of my head that had been screaming *Lucy, get out of here* since Scorpianne had brought her whip out suddenly got much louder. But I sat down, hoping my fear wasn't too obvious. She turned so that she was still looking at my reflection.

"What do you want, whore?" she said.

"I want to talk about Devil."

That was the wrong thing to say. Her face screwed up in an anguish so terrible, it looked like one of those Greek tragedy masks. "My brother!" she cried. "My little brother!"

I was overwhelmed. I hadn't expected such an emotional reaction. I had hoped I could talk to her reasonably, as I had talked to him; but she was too insane. Her smell began to make my head spin. It was like his, male in its essence, not female at all.

She was slow in getting herself under control, and that was even more terrible to watch. She kept her pale eyes on me the whole time, as if I were the focus of all of her hate, all of her pain. Finally she grinned, revealing filed teeth.

"Cunt," she said.

"Don't call me that."

"Whore."

"Scorpianne, your brother wanted his freedom, did you know that?"

She didn't answer.

"Have you been to a doctor since you left Mars?"

Her grin faded. For a moment she looked disoriented; she even started to put one hand to her head. But the very next moment I was sprawled flat on the floor with a brutal pain in the middle of my face where my nose used to be. She had squashed it like a tomato. She reached down and casually took my gun away, tossing it onto a couch across the room. Then she picked up her whip.

"You sell your cunt," she said. "You *are* a cunt."

"What are you then?" I gasped, my voice distorted into a nasal honk. "You sell pain."

She shook her head. "I don't sell pain. I give it away."

"I know a doctor who can help you—"

"Too late." Her face twisted, then went horribly blank. "You guessed wrong what I sell."

I cringed.

"Guess!" she ordered. "Guess again!"

"Scorpianne, don't—"

"Guess!!" she shrieked, thrusting her file-toothed face toward mine.

"What is it, then?!"

"Death!" She raised the whip handle over her head, triumphantly. "I kill for a living. Machine Co. is my customer tonight."

She let me have it with the whip. I felt it right through my protective suit. I scrambled out the door, trying to find a place to run. She followed.

"You should have taken the five-hundred thou," she said and struck me again. "Now I'll have it, along with the money that would have gone to your whore friends. Dead friends."

I stumbled to my feet and ran down the hall—the wrong way. The only thing at that end was a staircase, so of course I took it. She came inexorably after me and began to blast away at me with the whip in earnest.

I was dripping blood on the third flight of stairs. I was crawling by the fifth. But I kept going, and so did she, until we climbed past the eighth floor and came out onto the roof.

I backed away from her, all the way to the edge. She strolled after me.

"Tell me about Devil," she said eagerly, as if we were old friends having a chat.

I had to swallow a lot of blood and mucus before I could answer her.

"He wanted to be called John," I said.

"What?!"

"John Carter. After a character in his favorite books."

She looked very angry for a moment, then sad again. "I miss him. But I couldn't stand to see him."

"Why?" I said, still fighting for breath.

"*I* was supposed to be male, too. And red. I should have been like him, not like this. I could have had you if I had been like him."

"You can still have me, Scorpianne."

She frowned, but her whip hand seemed to relax, slightly.

"You made love to me once. With the Machine, remember?"

She kept her silence, but her breathing was becoming more like mine. Labored.

"I loved it. I loved what you did to me." I started to unzip what was left of my black jumpsuit. My breasts were unmarked by the whip. I exposed them, started to stroke them. Her eyes followed my hands, helplessly.

"Did you really like the way I danced for Rico?" I asked.

"—Yes—"

"I could do it for you. Do you have a dildo? One of those ones that stimulate your clitoris when you're fucking someone? You could wear that. I hope it's a big one."

"I know what you're trying to do."

"I'm a whore. I like it. You know what I am."

"You're the most beautiful woman in the world, Lucy."

I leaned against the edge of the roof, exhausted, vulnerable, my breasts thrust forward, since my face was now a ruined mess. She stumbled toward me, but she was raising the whip again.

"I'm going to kill you," she said, and struck at me for the last time.

I grabbed the whipcord, cutting my hands to the bone, and yanked hard.

Those hooves of hers weren't flexible. She clutched at me as she pitched forward, but I threw myself out of the way. She landed on her knees, still falling, and there was nothing she could grab to stop herself.

She tumbled over, fell eight floors, and landed with a CRUNCH.

I didn't look at her body. I just sat there and throbbed.

I wasn't happy that she was dead. She had been glorious. A glorious monster.

It took me years to get to my feet again. I aimed myself at the stairwell, but before I could reach it the

Machine Co. executive stepped out of the shadows and blocked my way.

"We would like to make a second offer," he said. He pulled a cashier's check out and extended it to me. I didn't touch it, but I read it.

It was for $2.7 million. The *Pay to the Order of* line wasn't filled in.

"This was supposed to be *her* check," I said.

"It was. It is now less expensive to pay you off than it is to hire a more competent assassin."

"Like the ones Ozma was growing?"

He shrugged.

"I don't want to get blood all over the check." I tugged my jumpsuit back over my shoulders and painfully zipped it up, my hands already stiffening up in permanent agony. "Put it in my breast pocket."

For the first time I saw some genuine and prolonged expression in his face. Distaste. But he did as I asked, his hand trembling at the brief contact.

"What do you think she was going to do with the money?" I asked him. "Get a sex change operation? Is that what you promised her?"

"It's not your concern. I assure you, Miss Cartier, it's too expensive to chase you anymore. That doesn't sit well with our marginal analysis. Our business with you is concluded."

"Thanks a lot, you bastard."

He didn't react to the insult, so I tried another.

"Machine Co. is failing, isn't it?"

He frowned.

"I heard some customers in the bar talking about how hard it is to unload their Machines. The bottom has fallen out of the market, and people can't *give* them away."

"You don't know what you're talking about," he sneered.

"You should have diversified. You dug your own graves."

"Nonsense. This new trend will turn around."

I spat blood on his shoes, and he cringed. "You idiot," I said. "You don't even know what the next thing is."

"Go to hell, you dumb bitch." He turned on his heel and marched toward the stairwell. I watched him go, helplessly. In another moment he would be down the stairs and out of sight. But he stopped at the head of the stair and jumped back. Someone was coming up.

"Excuse me," he snapped as a tall, lean shadow loomed over him. He made to slip past the figure, but it reached out and practically yanked him off his feet, pulling him close. It showed him something glittering and sharp in its hand.

"This is for the Machine that hurt my woman," said a familiar voice, and the knife hit Mr. Executive in the gut, right where his stomach would be. He curled around it in agony.

"And this is for the bomb in my shop." The knife went in again, this time with an explosion of air that might have been a gasp or might have been from another part of Mr. Executive's body.

"And this is for calling my Lucy a dumb bitch." Mr. Executive was dragged upright by his hair, and the knife went into his throat, just under his chin. I saw it poke out the other side, just to the left of his spinal column.

The executive died then, and he hit the ground, twitching.

Tiny electrical arcs glittered at me from black eyes. I tried to move, and the last of my energy drained out of me like water. But Joe was there to catch me before I fell.

"Lucy, why didn't you wait for me?" he choked. He sounded almost like Rico that way. His skin was still pale and gray from regeneration. He couldn't have been out for more than an hour; his long hair felt damp. I wanted to kiss him, but my mouth was caked with blood. I wanted to put my hands on his face, but they were open to the bone. So instead I rested the back of my hand on his cheek. His eyes went wide.

"You touched me," he said.

He picked me up as gently as he could, waiting for any sign of my old reaction, but getting none.

"Ann and my son are downstairs, *querida*. Can you wait a little while for doctoring?"

"Yes." I leaned my head against his shoulder and gazed into his new, perfect face.

"We'll fix you up, Lucy," he promised. "You'll have your pretty face back, I promise." He carried me down the stairs. The agony in my hands spread up my arms and down my spine, but I smiled.

"That son of a bitch had two guys waiting for you downstairs," he was saying. "Shit! You should have seen the looks on their faces when Rico and I—"

I thought how nice it would be to faint, then. It hurt so bad I could hardly believe it. But I was wide awake, through the long ride, and the doctoring, and everything.

Wide awake.

After Scorpianne was dead, trouble seemed to go far away from me and mine. It went to Mars, where the business consortium was disintegrating as new charges of fraud and murder surfaced almost daily. It went to Ganymede, where the miners had once again become fed up with conditions they should never have had to endure. It fermented and came to a boil, spilling over into the entire solar system, until finally it came back to Earth again.

Red Hulot called our house on Mykonos one lazy afternoon when I was preparing to take a walk on our private beach. He had good news and bad news.

"You can have your commission back if you want it," he told Rico. "There's just one catch."

"What is it?" asked Rico, unable to keep the hope from his voice. But Joe's face was deadpan. It had turned out to be easy to tell them apart after all, despite Joe's haircut.

"Once I told your ladyfriend there that the Jovian miners should have been given more concessions. You remember that, Lucy? You remember what you said back then?"

"I said they ought to go independent."

His sharp eyes glittered with anger and excitement.

"Damned straight. That's what they did. I knew this was going to happen. We're going to need every available pilot and mining technician from the inner system, and we're going to have to train a hell of a lot more."

"What is it?" demanded Rico.

"Four Atens hurtling out this way. That's no big deal, we can wrangle them, but six more are on the way. If they keep them coming like that, we're going to have all we can do just to divert them. We're going to be a lot busier than we can afford to be."

"Time to negotiate again," I said.

"Yeah, sure, but in the meantime—"

Ann appeared in the archway linking our living room and the study. "Mr. Hulot—"

"Is that Annie? Come where I can see you, girl."

That was pretty damned funny, considering Ann's real age. But she went to stand in front of the monitor. "Any sign of Ozma?" she asked.

"Not a trace. Can't even tell you if she's alive or dead. None of her old associates have heard from her, the ones who aren't in jail, I mean. Frankly, I think she's dead."

Ann nodded. I couldn't tell if that was an agreement or not.

"And the shock troops?"

"No sign of them either. No one has been killed mysteriously in the past two years, so we're assuming they were all destroyed in the original experiment. Officially, that is."

Officially. The news media still talked about the subject from time to time, along with other concerns, such as longevity, war, and bio-engineering.

"I want my commission back," said Rico, startling me. My heart squeezed in my chest, but I kept silent.

"I thought you might feel that way," Red grinned at him. "Can you leave in the morning?"

Rico said yes. My head started to ring, and I left the room before Red could tell me good-bye, before I could hear the rest of the arrangements.

A half hour later, Ann caught up with me on the beach.

"Joe's going too," she said.

"I knew he would."

We walked in silence for a long while, until Ann slowed me with a touch on my arm.

"The baby," she warned. She put her hand on her abdomen, where her child was swelling, five months along.

"I'm sorry." I took her hand and put my other arm around her waist, supporting her while we walked more slowly. The sun was pleasant. The sea was a vibrant turquoise, and if we let our imaginations roam just a little bit, we could see the mountains of the gods, just on the horizon where the sea met the sky.

I had been thinking only of myself. Now Rico was leaving before he would have a chance to see his and Ann's child born. I wondered if I would ever grow the kind of compassion I would need to be a decent partner in my family.

"I spoke to Doctor Kahn today," Ann said. "She's too intelligent, I'm afraid. She had many questions about the nanones."

"We knew it was coming," I said.

My sculpting practice had begun to earn me so much money I had recently hired a lawyer to help

me look after it. I now liaisoned with doctors in
Phoenix, LA, Chicago, New York, Milan, Buenos
Aires, Mexico City, Paris, and Athens. I could have
done so in other cities, too, if I could just learn to
give up sleep.

"I don't blame myself for it," Ann said. "I don't
even blame Ozma. Plenty of researchers have been
working in this field—I wouldn't be here today if it
weren't for Dr. Chin, three hundred years ago . . ."

"You told Kahn your age?" I said. That seemed
unwise.

"No."

I glanced at her, hearing trouble in her voice. Her
brow was creased, her eyes haunted.

"How long will Rico and Joe be gone?" I asked
gently.

"Five years, at least. But what difference does it
make when you live forever?"

Forever. I hadn't heard that word yet in reference
to our own personal situations. Rico had consented
to have tissue samples frozen so he could regenerate
new organs when they were needed, and we were
all on Ann's new viruses. But she hadn't said *that*
word until now.

Someone was walking an erratic path up the beach
toward us, running out to the water and then re-
treating and laughing gaily as it chased him back
inland. I could see nothing of him but his pale,
creamy skin and bright red hair. But as I got closer
I could see he was wearing a headband of some sort.
He might be Hermes, the eternal boy.

He saw us and waved. We waved back.

"Kahn asked me a disturbing question," Ann said.
"We had been talking about age limits. She came

right out and asked me what I thought they might be. I was conservative. I told her there was no reason a person couldn't live to be two hundred or more. I was prepared to give her my speech about quality of life and that sort of thing. But she cut me right off. She said, 'What about the children?' "

I waited to hear what was significant about that, but Ann was done talking. I hadn't thought much about the question, myself. I had assumed people would start having children less often. After all, if you had the choice of waiting until you were fifty or even a hundred, wouldn't you take it? Both Joe and Rico had asked me to bear them a child. I had promised to do it within the next decade. But did I really mean it? Did I really *want* it?

I watched the boy running back and forth to the water. He looked to be about nine years old. Nine was a good age for joy, for living life just for the water and the sunshine. Could I ever feel the way that boy was feeling? Could I shed my adult body and be a child? Ozma had.

"We're the children, Ann," I said. "We're the future."

She shivered in my arms. The boy ran across the sand until he was no more than ten feet away from us. He turned his lovely face into the sunshine, and the ornament at its center turned a molten color, red and gold. It was two letters, which burned themselves into my retinas. They were O and Z, interlocking.

OZ.

The boy scooped up two handsful of sand and let them pour between his fingers. Did I see something else glittering there, under the sand? But no, his eyes were shining, green jewels that invited us in, promising us an endless future.

We had no choice but to accept.

ROC (0451)

ISAAC ASIMOV BRINGS THE UNIVERSE TO YOU

☐ **THE BEST SCIENCE FICTION OF ISAAC ASIMOV by Isaac Asimov.** Here is a collection of 28 "best ever personal favorites" from the short works of the master of science fiction, featuring brief introductions to each story by the author. "Illustrates the amazing versatility and endless originality of Isaac Asimov."—*Booklist* (450698—$3.99)

☐ **ROBOT VISIONS by Isaac Asimov.** From the Grandmaster of science fiction, 36 magnificent stories and essays about his most beloved creations—the robots. And these "robot visions" are skillfully captured in illustrations by Academy Award-winner Ralph McQuarrie, production designer of *Star Wars*. (450647—$5.99)

Prices slightly higher in Canada.

MAGICAL REALMS

☐ **LADIES** *Retold Tales of Goddesses and Heroines* **by Boris and Doris Vallejo.** In this dazzling melding of verbal and visual artistry, Doris reveals profound truths about the women and men behind the legends. This is a masterpiece which includes 10 new paintings and a multitude of drawings by Boris, art work that combines with Doris's evocative and lyrical language to form a fitting celebration of Women of Power. (451074—$18.00)
Hardcover: (452070-$35.00)

☐ **THE LAST UNICORN by Peter S. Beagle.** One of the most beloved tales in the annals of fantasy—the spellbinding saga of a creature out of legend on a quest beyond time. (450523—$8.00)

☐ **A FINE AND PRIVATE PLACE by Peter S. Beagle.** Illustrated by Darrell Sweet. Michael and Laura discovered that death did not have to be an end, but could be a beginning. A soul-stirring, witty and deeply moving fantasy of the heart's desire on both sides of the dark divide. (450965—$9.00)

Prices slightly higher in Canada

If you and/or a friend would like to receive the *ROC Advance*, a bimonthly newsletter featuring all the newest and hottest ROC books and authors, on a complimentary basis, please fill out this form and return it to:

ROC Books/Penguin USA
375 Hudson Street
New York, NY 10014

Your Address
Name _____
Street _____ Apt. # _____
City _____ State _____ Zip _____

Friend's Address
Name _____
Street _____ Apt. # _____
City _____ State _____ Zip _____